A Fool's Errand

By

Jim Beegle

This book is lovingly dedicated to my Father & Mother

Thank you for giving me the wisdom to deal with the things I encountered on a daily basis, and the hope to always look ahead.

Author's Notes:

A Fool's Errand was in the back of my mind the whole time I was writing ***Purely By Accident,*** my first book. After it was published, my friends and readers started asking me "what next?" I went back and pulled out my notes and started writing again.

I learned a lot writing ***Purely By Accident*** and I hope the lessons come through in ***A Fool's Errand***. One of the things I learned was just how much I hate editing and how important a good editor is to my books, especially with my somewhat loose grasp of the English language. As I finished writing a chapter I would put it through a grammar check program that would always recommend I try their Klingon version first.

As with my first book writing ***A Fool's Errand*** has been a collaborative effort, more so this time I think. I am a lucky fellow to have so many friends willing to help and advise me. My name is on the cover, but it really is ours in spirit if not truth.

Many thanks to:

Karen Holt, for doing the wonderful job she did editing, reading my mind, and not letting me get away with anything.

Kate Myers, for editing, suggestions, and encouragement.

Dawn Goll, for post edits review, suggestions, and always cheering me on.

Mike & Alta - Calvin & Martha for helping me through the hard times and making the good times that much better.

Susan Kellogg, for helping to make sure I was around to write a second novel.

Kay & William Roberts, for book jacket and website photos.

Alphie and Aunt Agnus, for making sure it took twice as long as it should have to get finished.

Books by Jim Beegle

Purely By Accident - www.purelybyaccident.com

A Fool's Errand - www.afoolserrand.net

Table of Contents

CHAPTER ONE 1

CHAPTER TWO 9

CHAPTER THREE 29

CHAPTER FOUR 41

CHAPTER FIVE 63

CHAPTER SIX 77

CHAPTER SEVEN 87

CHAPTER EIGHT 103

CHAPTER NINE 115

CHAPTER TEN 123

CHAPTER ELEVEN 137

CHAPTER TWELVE 155

CHAPTER THIRTEEN 163

CHAPTER FOURTEEN 173

CHAPTER FIFTEEN 189

CHAPTER SIXTEEN 195

A Fool's Errand

CHAPTER ONE

The Royal Palace – Thebes, Lower Egypt (1323 BC)

The floods would not come this year.

That's what the stupid priests had told him months ago. Now, it appeared the old fools were right. Tutankhamun was not sure which infuriated him more; the fact the floods had not come or that the priests had been right about it.

Only one of many but, the primary task of the priests of the Temple of Amun-Ra, was to inform The Pharaoh when the annual flooding of the Nile would occur. The priests predict the floods, which enabled all of the upper and lower valleys of the Nile to plant crops to feed the people, provide for the livestock of the country, and ensure the continued prosperity of Egypt.

Now the priests had informed him the floods would not come and they had not. This on top of last year when the floods had come but not as abundantly as they had in the past and not enough for both last year and this, meant less grain in the storehouses of the Pharaoh.

Tutankhamun paced and slapped the horsehair-topped scepter into his open palm as he limped back and forth in his private throne room. The young king was troubled not because he feared for his people, but because he feared the people; especially when the price of grain reached beyond the purse of his average subject before the grain completely ran out. Hungry people could easily turn into an unruly mob.

Trouble seemed to plague him at every turn, and it was the fault of the priests of Amun.

He had done much for the priests within the span of his short reign to satisfy these stupid old men. He had ruled Akhenaten, his father, was wrong to abandon Amun-Ra as one of the main gods of Egypt for the single god of the solar disc; Aten.

He had restored the capital from Karnak, where his father, Akhenaten, had moved it to facilitate the worship of Aten back to Thebes and restored the temple of Amun-Ra in Luxor. And this is how they chose to repay his kindness.

Even though his father had purged Egypt of the priests of Amun-Ra and defaced their temples once Tutankhamun had gained the throne they returned en masse. Like jackals lurking in the shadows on the outer edge of the lion's kill, the priests of Amun-Ra had moved in quickly once the danger had passed to feast and brag that is was, they who had hunted and brought down the prey instead of the lioness. They strutted and spoke as if they, and not he, Tutankhamun, had restored Thebes to its rightful place in Egypt.

Now the panic over the damnable river had worked its way into the palace. His advisors and family, even his stepmother, Nefertiti, worried him constantly about what was to be done about the fact the Nile would not flood this year. What did they expect? Did he command the Nile?

Pharaoh must do this, or Pharaoh must do that they told him. Like flies buzzing around a dung pile they were constantly speaking of nothing but the river that would not flood.

Even so, these priests, these dung flies, had persuaded him to allocate many of the servants of his palace and a great deal of the wealth of his Treasury into a plan to dig a massive tunnel below the receding water line of the Nile into the cities and farms along the river. Once completed, the final measure of the earth holding back the diminished Nile would be removed to allow the waters to flow through the tunnel diverting even more water out of the river.

They wasted his time and patience over the river and their schemes seemed designed not to move water but to consume his days and most of the Treasury.

Was he not the warrior son of his father? Was he not to grow the power and influence of Egypt through the conquest of other lands and peoples? How then was the Treasury to be refilled if he did not take tribute from the conquered wealth of those he defeated in battle?

Instead of doing what his destiny demanded he should do and lead his army in wars of conquest and glory for Egypt and for his legacy, he instead spent his daily measures of the Sun listening to worried women and nattering priests about the flooding of the Nile, demanding he divert vast amounts of his resources into moving dirt to accommodate the whim of the river.

The people depended on Pharaoh to ensure there was water for the crops so there would be grain in the markets, the priests told him. And if there was no flood, would the priests themselves take responsibility for not offering the right kind and number of sacrifices?

No, they would claim they had done everything within their powers to bring prosperity to the land of Egypt. The gods must be offended beyond their ability to pacify them. Instead, they would blame Pharaoh for angering the gods of Egypt. Oh, they would not come out and say so directly in the temples.

They would whisper it in the marketplaces. They would speak of it amongst themselves and their closest associates. One would tell another, in the strictest confidence, of course, until the whole of Egypt would declare that Pharaoh had offended the gods and caused the rains not to fall and the Nile not to rise.

"Pharaoh?" Tutankhamun spun to see who dared invade his personal chambers without his leave.

"Pharaoh?" Nefertiti asked again. She paused as he turned to face her. Seeing the anger in his face, she knelt and crossed herself, realizing she had gone beyond the boundaries of her authority in the palace by invading Tutankhamun's private chambers.

As Queen, the wife of Akhenaten, she often considered herself exempt from the edicts of her young stepson although she was fully aware, she was not allowed to enter this part of the palace without requesting permission of him beforehand. Today, however, was not the day to disregard that her husband's son was the Pharaoh of Egypt.

Tutankhamun reluctantly extended his scepter towards the woman as a sign of his permission to stay. Without such an acknowledgment the Pharaoh's personal guards, who were unseen but omnipresent, would seize and remove Nefertiti from Pharaoh's sight.

Tutankhamun did not speak but held his stepmother in his disapproving gaze.

"Pharaoh," she began again, "I have come from the temple of Amun the priests…" Tutankhamun cut her off.

"And what doom do these men who worry like old widows begging in the market have to say today?"

"My son…," Tutankhamun cut her off again.

"Woman," he said with cold anger in his voice, "You may be the wife of my father, and rightfully a Queen of Egypt, but," he paused and bore his gaze into her, "I am not your son."

Anger at this insult flashed through Nefertiti, but she quickly recovered control of herself. It was wrong that this child, so spoiled and pampered, should be the Pharaoh of all of Egypt. Today, however, was not the day to challenge the power this boy held. She lowered her eyes to the floor.

"As always Pharaoh, you are right. I, like all of Egypt, am yours to command," she said in submission. Satisfied that he had put her, at least for now, in her proper place Tutankhamun turned, walked to his throne, and seated himself.

"And what do these gossiping old women, these dung flies have to predict today?" He finally asked her.

"Pharaoh is it wise to say such things of the priests of the gods of Egypt?" she asked.

"Wise or not, it is the truth." He sighed. "Tell me and be quick about it, what is their demand of Pharaoh this time?"

"The tunnel being dug is near completion. They advise you flood it as soon as possible before the Nile recedes any further." The boy considered this for a quick moment, and then clapped his hands twice.

From seemingly out of nowhere, a young man appeared, bowing at the waist before the boy seated on the throne.

"You have heard what the Queen has asked of Pharaoh?" The young man nodded his head once.

"Then record the word of the Pharaoh's decision that now is the time to flood the tunnel dug from the Nile."

Using a pointed reed, the young man quickly inscribed the tablet in his hand. When this was finished, he bowed on one knee before the boy on the throne, extending the tablet towards Pharaoh.

Tutankhamun removed the signet ring from his finger, the oracle of the Pharaoh passed down to him by his father, Akhenaten, and pressed it into the pliable clay of the tablet.

"Let the word of Pharaoh, as it is so written, be known to the priests," he said with a dismissive wave of his hand. The young man rose and left quickly. Turning his attention to his stepmother, he spoke.

"Are there other needs you have of Pharaoh?" He asked her.

"Would it not be prudent oh Pharaoh to be seen at the Nile as the tunnel is opened?" She inquired. "Maybe to grant an offering to the Nile to ensure the people that Pharaoh is concerned about the flooding?" Tutankhamun groaned as he rose from his throne and limped to the open balcony overlooking the river.

"No, it would not," he said firmly. "I have just this morning instructed my captain to have my barque made ready for a trip up the Nile. I have too long neglected a visit to my father's tomb, and I have need to inspect the preparation for my own place of departure to the River Aaru."

"Is it wise to leave now when the people are so worried about the Nile? They draw strength from you when they know you share their concerns for the harvest," she said to her stepson; knowing full well her protest would only strengthen his resolve to go.

"There are many demands on Pharaoh. I am weary of the worries of the priests and since they have declared the floods will not come this year, I will need to travel while there is still water in the Nile on which to float," he said without turning to face her.

"As always, I am sure the wisdom of Pharaoh is best. Grant now my leave, Pharaoh, that I might be about your service elsewhere." Still without turning around, he waved his dismissal of the woman. She turned and walked across the room towards the exit.

Good, she thought to herself as she entered the open courtyard. While her arrogant stepson was off on his fool's errand to supervise the construction of his own tomb, she could move freely about and plan for his reception when he returned.

Her anger towards Tutankhamun grew as she walked across the courtyard. Did he not know that she had called upon the newly discovered power of the light to ensure his ascendency to rule as Pharaoh of all of Egypt? She, with the help of Horemheb, had marshaled this power to bring down the foolishness of Akhenaten and his single god worship of Aten.

She alone had been approached by the priests of Amun, and revealed the power of the light, unknown in Egypt before that time. They were persecuted by Akhenaten, their temples defaced, and their livelihood cut off.

It was in their desperation they approached her and revealed their most guarded secret; the power that could turn night into day. Not only the power, but its source as well, and where in all of Egypt it could be found. When applied properly the new weapon would race across the sands of the desert and burn with fire everything in its path.

She had counseled the priests as to how to use this power to bring down the Pharaoh and place one sympathetic to Amun back on the throne of Egypt. The priests had done as they were instructed. Tutankhamun had replaced Akhenaten.

For a while, the boy had listened to her and done as she had suggested. But now he listened to others, or in most cases, made decisions relying on his own counsel. He relished the office of Pharaoh and enjoyed the trappings of his office without acknowledging those who had brought him to the throne. He did not realize that the power of Pharaoh was invested in him only as he served others.

Especially Nefertiti.

By the time she reached the other side of the courtyard her fists were clinched in rage at her recent treatment by her stepson. She stopped and took a deep breath before she entered the other side of the palace. It would do no good to let her anger boil over and be visible to others. She relaxed her hands and composed herself before continuing on.

Anger would not serve her now. She had too much to do and must think with a clear head. She must find Horemheb and together they would go to see the high priests of Amun. It was time once more to solicit their help.

Only then, when he returned to the palace, after his trip up the Nile would Tutankhamun realize how prudent it had been for him to be concerned about his place of burial.

CHAPTER TWO

Valley of the Kings – Luxor Governorate, Egypt (Modern Day)

The warmth raced well ahead of the light announcing the start of another day. Jake Bracken could feel the heat quickly working through the thin canvas that made up the walls of his tent. In a matter of minutes, the temperature inside would soar to uncomfortable levels. Already it was too warm inside the sleeping bag he had rolled out on the foldout cot.

Once the light of the day retreated, chasing the Sun in a never-ending race westward, the desert temperature would plunge low enough to require blankets, or in Bracken's case a down sleeping bag.

He could already hear voices outside as the day laborers gathered to await instruction for the day's work. Still dressed in the jeans and long sleeve white cotton shirt he had been wearing when he fell into bed just four hours earlier, Jake unzipped the bag from the inside and sat up in the open shell it formed. Reaching under the cot he pulled out a pair of hiking boots made from smooth, but well-worn leather on top of heavy lugged rubber soles.

He turned each shoe over and shook it vigorously. Having spent time in the desert before, he was used to the morning dressing ritual of extricating the small snakes and scorpions that find nighttime warmth inside your footwear. Satisfied that nothing had taken up residence in his boots overnight he slipped his feet into them, grabbed the jacket laying on the foot of the bed, opened the flap of the tent and stepped outside into the morning.

No longer hindered by the six-foot ceiling of his canvas quarters, he stretched out to his full 6-foot 3-inch height, reaching for the clear, cloudless blue sky while letting out a groan of pleasure at the exercise. He looked around and took in the view of his surroundings. No matter how many times he looked upon the Valley of the Kings, he was always awed and amazed. He could not help but feel insignificant in the presence of history that covered centuries.

The walls of the canyons that comprised the Valley of the Kings were already reflecting the building heat of the day into the shaded areas where his campsite was set up. Egypt was in the middle of a hundred-year drought. In a land that had depended for centuries on the cycles of wet and dry, this extended drought was punishing the land, the people and the livestock. Wells and watering holes were drying up. If rain did not come soon, the water level of the Nile River, the nexus of the people since the time before the Pharaohs, would be so low that even barge traffic would be banned. Bracken turned his attention back to his surroundings and looked again as far as he could see over the rough terrain.

Thousands of years had passed over this wide and desolate valley, yet it was still one of the most mysterious places on earth. Every archeologist and student who had ever worked in the valley came away feeling the same way; there was so much more yet to discover, in addition to the years it would take to catalog and study the wealth of items already uncovered; or rather what was left.

Even before the tombs were sealed, grave robbers, drawn by the promise of unimaginable riches, began desecrating the resting-place of the Pharaohs. As dictated by his or her complex religion, each ruler was buried with a great collection of his personal wealth. It

was considered a serious blunder to arrive in the afterlife
with only chariot fare. That was one of the reasons the
Valley of the Kings came to be what it is today. Men who
were loyal to the departed rulers spirited away their
bodies and riches to this non-descript part of the
Egyptian desert, so as to prevent grave robbers from
carting off the Treasury of the Kings.

Bracken turned his attention to his more
immediate surroundings and scanned the close-in
landscape until he spotted a group of Iranian workers
huddled around a small cooking fire, they had started
from wood brought from their camp that morning. The
men talked in fast, animated tones as they squatted
facing the small fire.

He extracted a pipe and worn black tobacco pouch
from the pocket of his jacket as he walked towards the
gathering. They glanced at him as he joined the
periphery of their loose circle.

The conversation did not stop or even slow as
Jake squatted on his haunches like the other men and
pulled a flaming twig from the edge of the fire to light his
pipe. When he replaced the ember, the man closest to
him put a metal cup in his hand and poured hot tea from
a battered kettle that had been heating in the fire.

The tea was a kind Bracken had only been
exposed to in the Middle East. It was Indian, black and
strong. After the leaves were boiled, the liquid was
mixed with raw coarse sugar until it approached the
consistency of syrup.

Bracken nodded and told the man thank you in
one of only two phrases he knew in Farsi, the language
spoken in Iran. Iranians were the labor force en masse in
Egypt.

Like Mexicans in Texas, Iranians did the hard-
manual labor that took a strong body and little else. They

came to Egypt not to escape political or religious oppression; they came to the Arabian Desert for a more basic reason to escape from their homeland where there were too few jobs for too many men. This dig had a labor force of almost 30 men, primarily Iranians, but a few were Arabs from either Egypt or Jordan.

Jake smoked and drank his tea without any other contribution to or from the gathering. Bracken was a tall man, crowding his mid-forties. His face was open and friendly, and it was easy to see that the wear and tear to it was caused by extremes of heat and cold, as well as all the moderations in-between.

His mouth was outlined by a neatly trimmed mustache and goatee. His head was covered with medium brown hair revealing growing evidence of gray; it was shorter than it needed to be to lay down under its own weight and gave the appearance that it had never been trained to do anything its owner wished. All in all, he looked like an average guy.

He was not strikingly handsome or dashing; most people wouldn't give him a second look if they have met in a supermarket or in line at a movie theater. That is, unless they happened to look at his eyes, which he hid behind round silver wire-rimmed glasses.

They sparkled from a light that was ignited from the inside, smoldering with passion and confidence that belied the rest of his appearance. The irises were hazel and would shift from the brown end of the color spectrum to the green side, depending on the level of mischief that played through his mind. His eyes missed nothing that went on around him, but they were more than just portals for observation; he often used them to probe beyond the surface of the subject they engaged.

He finished his tea and handed the tin cup back to the man on his right. Turning his attention once more to

the pipe he repacked the tobacco and was in the process
of lighting it again when he heard an explosion that
rattled the ground slightly and raced with dense
compression through the dry warming air.

It was not a particularly loud blast, but it seemed
foreign and out of place amidst the hum of the workers'
conversations and the milling of the local livestock.
Equally odd was the fact no one seemed to give it more
than passing notice.

His body now caffeinated and the first smoke of
the day complete, Jake retreated to his tent for his toiletry
kit to complete the rest of his morning rituals. When he
reemerged from the tent, he noticed a man looking his
way and walking in his direction.

"Sorry, did I wake you?" Leon Platte asked Jake
without the slightest hint of concern in his voice as he got
within speaking distance. Leon was easily the opposite
in terms of physical appearance to Jake.

His body tapered inward from his shoulders to his
feet. He was just under six feet tall but made up in brawn
what he lacked in Bracken's height.

Working in their different roles at Solaris had
caused the two men's paths to cross on more than one
occasion. In fact, a number of the tales told around the
water coolers in Solaris' headquarters in Dallas involved
the exploits of Bracken and Platte.

Leon had accompanied Jake from Cairo two days
earlier to deliver Ground Penetrating Radar (GPR)
equipment on loan to the American's leading the project
from their employer; Solaris Oil Company.

Jake had piloted the plane with the equipment
while Leon had spent the last two days setting it up,
calibrating it and showing an assortment of graduate
students how to use it.

Ground Penetrating Radar involved firing a small blank mortar shell into the ground to set up a series of expanding seismic pulses. As the radiating energy struck objects in the ground, they bounced back a return energy wave that was collected by the radar system and analyzed by computer software written to specifically identify objects within the ground.

It was ordinarily used by Solaris to help locate oil and gas reserves hidden deep within the earth. However, the American-led archeological team was using the system in an attempt to locate lost burial tombs. Or so the Chairman of Solaris Oil, Marcus Coleman, had told Jake after receiving a call from a friend of his, who just happened to be the President of The University of Texas-Dallas, the organization running the project.

Jake was still unsure why he and Leon had to drag themselves and the equipment halfway around the globe for a bunch of pointy-headed academics.

"Because," Mr. Coleman told him over the phone, "that bunch of pointy-headed academics, as you call them, are friends of mine, not to mention the fact Solaris is a major contributor and underwriter of the project."

So, in other words, Jake thought to himself after hanging up, I am off on yet another fool's errand because you say so.

Mr. Coleman knew Jake would do as he asked. He also knew Bracken's grousing was just part of his nature, especially when Bracken was required to do something that required a lot of just sitting around, which both he and Bracken knew hauling Leon and the radar to the deserts of Egypt would entail.

"No," he answered his co-worker and friend. "Sorry to ruin your morning fun." He pointed an arm back towards the direction Leon had just come from. "How's it going?"

"Don't you mean, when can we get out of this godforsaken place?" Platte asked with a wicked smile. Bracken replied with a shrug.

"Either one is fine with me."

"Well, you are indeed in luck, as I will answer both questions." He said with a sweeping gesture of his hand and a slight bow. "The kids have the system down pat. They don't need me here anymore. Which should answer your second question as well." Bracken did not immediately react but stood there thinking. Finally, he turned to Platte.

"If we hurry, we can have dinner in Paris tonight." He said with a wide grin.

"And you're buying." It was more of a statement than a question.

"Screw that," Bracken answered patting his back-left pocket where he kept his wallet and Solaris credit card. "We'll let Mr. Coleman buy."

"Oh," Platte replied with a grin to match Bracken's. "In that case, I'll get packed." Before the sound of their voices died in the warming morning air, they became aware of a commotion coming from the general direction that Platte had just come from.

The hubbub was immediately followed by a mixed crowd of day labors and gang foremen moving towards Platte and Bracken at a harried pace. Bracken could see shock and fear in the ashen faces and wide eyes of the men as they streamed past him.

Even though Jake understood little if any of the words being exchanged, he recognized the tone. They spoke in loud hurried voices like the ones Jake recalled using as a kid when he would have to walk in the pitch-dark back to the main house from the barn. The louder your voice, even if you were only talking to yourself, the braver you felt; or so it seemed at the time.

Behind the first cluster came a second comprised of the Egyptians and others connected with directing the dig. Some of them Bracken recognized as a unit Platte had been working with for the past few days, learning to use the equipment he had flown into the site.

They moved in smaller groups and spoke in hushed, almost reverent tones. Some displayed the same wide eyes and ashen face of the group that had preceded them. The remainder of the second group radiated shock, but their expression was comprised of worry rooted in deep personal concern. When Platte looked at Bracken, Jake knew he had seen the same thing in the faces of the men as they rushed past. He raised his dark black eyebrow before turning to the men just passing in front of them.

"Dr. Rashid," Platte called to one of the men he recognized. A tall, thin man with a dark complexion turned at the sound of his name. Platte walked towards him with Bracken in tow.

Dr. Rashid excused himself from the tight clutch of men he had been traveling with and met Leon about halfway from where they had started.

"Please, my friend," Platte began respectfully in hopes of putting the man at ease.

"There seems to be a great commotion. What has happened, has there been a discovery?" But Leon knew from the look on this man face and the others, that whatever had been discovered was not good and, had scared the living daylights out of a whole company of grown men.

"It is most disturbing," began Dr. Rashid, "most troubling. Dr. Mohammed did not show up this morning as we began our work. We were continuing from where we finished yesterday so we began without him. As more time passed, we became concerned, as this was not his custom to be so late for the important work, he was responsible for," he told the two men from Solaris.

A man from the University of Texas, Dr. Lester Walker, was actually managing the dig itself. But each site was assigned a coordinator from the Egyptian government's Department of History and Antiquities, who saw to it that the requirements of the Egyptian Government were adhered to dealing with their country's past. Dr. Mohammed was that man for this project.

Nothing could be done at any site unless he approved it first. Dr. Rashid was his assistant and charged with most, if not all, of the day-to-day oversight and review of what the American team was doing and where they were doing it.

"We sent someone to find him and discovered him they thought, still asleep, in his tent." The man paused and trembled. "His assistant tried to awaken him but found him dead." Leon started to ask something else but then noticed the man had only paused in his narrative.

"When the young man looked at his face, it was contorted, as if he had been overtaken by some great fear."

The manner in which Dr. Rashid described his colleague's condition convinced both Americans he had witnessed the scene firsthand.

"The day workers are concerned. They are convinced that the spirit of the Pharaoh or perhaps even Ra himself, has been angered by what we are doing and have sent either a curse or an avenger to show their displeasure," Dr. Rashid said in detachment. Bracken then joined the conversation for the first time.

"Surely you don't believe in the curse of the Pharaohs?" Jake asked in a gentle tone, allowing room for the man to say that he did have such a belief.

"I am an educated man," the Egyptian said, looking at Bracken, "but I do not know how to explain the death of my colleague. He was not an old man, and to the best of my personal knowledge, in good health." He paused for a moment, as if coming to a decision.

"I will wait and see what the proper authorities conclude about this matter before I make up my mind. As to the curse, of course, I do not believe in such things." The learned man turned to leave but added to his reply.

"However, this is the Valley of the Kings, the resting place of the great rulers of Egypt, who were believed to be gods themselves. Who can know what power the gods might still possess in this place?"

Leon watched the man trot off to find his living companions. He turned to say something to Bracken, but Jake cut him off.

"Get your gear and let's get moving," Bracken told him in a hurried tone.

"I don't…." Platte began, but Jake cut him off again.

"If you and I don't get in the air and out of Egyptian airspace before the cops get here, they're going to ground the plane and detain us," Bracken said, looking at his watch.

"I am not afraid of the authorities I have no desire to sit here watching the sun bake the sand while the Egyptian version of Colombo interviews everyone at the scene of the crime."

It didn't take Platte more than a second to understand what his friend was trying to tell him. They made arrangements to meet in half an hour at their plane, which was sitting on the dirt strip airfield a few miles from where they stood. It almost worked as Bracken had planned. Right up to the point of arriving at the plane to find it already under the watchful eye of the Egyptian National Police.

No amount of discussion could change anyone's mind. Just as Bracken had feared, they were stranded, as minor players in the investigation into the death of Dr. Mohammed.

By the time both men made it back to the campsite the body had been removed and the inquiry into the events leading up to the death was underway. In time the authorities interviewed both Bracken and Platte.

Both men were asked to account for their time and movements during the day and evening during the previous day. It was a straightforward process.

Questions were politely asked, and answers politely given. In addition, they were asked about the others in the group, and they knew that others were being questioned as to Bracken and Platte's whereabouts as well.

No one was describing what was going on as anything other than routine. But as with most routines, it was interesting only when it was your turn to participate. Once his interview was over, Bracken found himself with too much time on his hands and nothing to keep him occupied.

He called Mr. Coleman's secretary in Dallas to let someone at Solaris know what was going on. When that was done, he thought about simply taking a nap, but he knew the heat would make sleeping impossible. He finally decided to walk to the airfield and pre-flight the airplane in hopes of being able to leave sooner rather than later.

This way he could take his time and give the plane a careful inspection. As he walked to the airstrip, he recalled the rule that all pilots everywhere lived by when it came to pre-flighting a plane. There are old pilots, and there are bold pilots, but there are no old, bold pilots. Besides, he thought as he walked towards the airfield, it gave him something to do to pass the time.

Bracken walked about a mile before coming to the short, three-quarter mile-long airstrip that had been packed into the sand close to the main camping area. There was a collection of odd and assorted support equipment sitting around along with some small single-engine planes used to ferry people and supplies out from Cairo.

Without any doubt, however the view of the airfield was dominated by the brightly polished aluminum DC3 with the large yellow and red Solaris logo on the side.

The size of the airfield here dictated Bracken's choice of the plane he brought into the Valley. With a short field, the DC3 was the perfect plane to use for the task. But even if the airfield weren't restricted in runway length, Bracken would have still picked "The Three", as it was fondly known.

He loved flying the old plane.

First put into service in December 1937, it was built by the Douglas Aircraft Company at the behest of C.R. Smith, the then-infamous president of what later became American Airlines. Smith wanted a plane that was larger and more luxurious than the aircraft in service at the time.

Most of those planes were originally designed as military aircraft of one sort or another. The Three was the first plane built specifically to carry paying passengers. It had a range of 1,500 miles and lumbered along at only 175 miles per hour, fast for its day, but woefully slow in the modern jet-age.

Even though it was first built for the fledgling commercial airline industry, it also tendered service with air forces all over the world. Its last US military use was as late as the Vietnam War where it was outfitted with automatic air-cooled Gatling guns that could deliver thousands of rounds a minute.

It was nicknamed "Puff The Magic Dragon" or "Puff" for short, by the ground troops it supported. It could lay down such a concentration of fire that any wooded area attacked ended up looking like a team of professional loggers had stripped it. Bracken loved the plane for two reasons.

The first was that it was a fly-by-wire aircraft, meaning the controls of the plane, the steering yoke and rudders were directly connected to the control surfaces by miles of steel cable.

A pilot could detect a change in the way an engine was running just from the feedback vibrations coming through the steering yoke, telegraphed there by the steel control cables running throughout the body of the plane.

The second reason was the very reason that most people disliked it; it flew low and slow. Bracken loved to see the landscape he was flying over. Faster, higher-flying aircraft did not afford him the pleasure of sticking his head out the cockpit window to check to see if the landing gear was down when he made his final approach to an airport. It was a plane built for people who loved to fly planes, not for people in a hurry to get somewhere.

But it was also a tricky plane to takeoff and land. It required skills long since lost on the younger brace of pilots.

The Three was a taildragger. It did not have the standard tricycle configuration front and body landing gear of most planes. It had the body gear like all the others but instead of a set of wheels under the nose, it had a small swiveling tail wheel.

Unlike landing a modern plane, you had to float The Three down dead level, so the main body wheel touched first before the plane settled down on the rear swivel gear. It required a pilot with real flying skills, not a computer-assisted bus driver like the 737 pilots flying for Southwest Airlines.

Bracken unlocked and opened the side door and quickly made his way to the cockpit. Once there, he switched on the batteries and then powered up the older, but still serviceable electronics.

He checked all the gauges to make sure they were working properly, and then checked to see what they were recording about the rest of the plane. Satisfied that all was well with the instrumentation he turned it all off before going to have a look around the outside of the plane.

Before exiting he fished out a pair of worn leather gloves and a large metal flashlight, out from a storage box under the navigator's chart table.

He left through the same door he had come in and replaced his wire-rimmed glasses with a pair of aviator's sunglasses. He spent the next hour probing the engine, landing gear and control surfaces with the flashlight. He finalized his inspection by climbing out on the wing, and visually checking the level of 115/145 Avgas in the fuel tanks.

By the time he climbed down off the wing the ever-rising heat of the day had caused the perspiration from his body to soak his shirt. He leaned into the fuselage of the plane and stuck the flashlight into a cracked leather pouch riveted to the plane's body just inside the open hatch.

He was locking the plane up when he heard a jeep arrive on the other side of the aircraft. Bracken was making his way around the plane when he heard his name called out loudly.

"I'm right here," he called, as he came into sight of the jeep. The man doing the shouting was a Sargent in the national police. He was standing up in the passenger seat of the vehicle and looking in the direction of the cockpit window until he heard Bracken's voice. The driver, a man of lower rank looked bored as he stared forward through the sand coated windshield.

"Mr. Bracken?" Jake just nodded his acknowledgment. "Ah, your friend Mr. Platte said we might find you here." The policemen's English was perfect. Jake could tell it had been learned from someone who spoke British-style and not American-style English.

"Is there a problem?' Bracken asked. The relaxed manner of the policeman told Jake there was not, but it was still reassuring to hear it confirmed.

"No, sir. We have concluded our investigation and you are free to go about your business. As I departed your camp, your associate, Mr. Platte, asked if I would stop here on my way back to the city and let you know this information." Jake nodded to the man again.

"Thank you, Sargent. Was there an arrest in the case?"

"No, sir. The medical examiner has assured us that we were not dealing with a murder." The officer told Jake.

"That is a relief," Bracken said, truly meaning it. "What was the cause of Dr. Mohammed's death?" At this, the policeman screwed up his face in almost pure agony.

"That is still the mystery. The good Doctor did not die from foul play, but the medical examiner is unable to determine the exact cause of death. He just ceased to live."

Bracken recalled the description of the dead man's face Dr. Rashid had conveyed to him. It did not jive with what he was hearing, and he started to say so to the officer until caution came to his rescue.

"I'm sure, given time you will discover all you need to know," was all Bracken said to the man. The police Sargent agreed with the Solaris pilot and wished him a good journey as he resettled himself into the seat of the jeep.

Bracken stood for a moment watching them drive across the dirt airstrip before turning to make his way back to camp.

During the walk back to camp he removed the gloves and stuffed them into the back pocket of his jeans creating the appearance of a farmer coming in from the fields. He had not gone far before he cursed himself for neglecting to bring a cap to keep the sun off his head and face.

As he reached the campsite, he saw Platte standing in front of his tent talking with the director of the project, Dr. Lester Walker, and his assistant, Dr. Kate Compton.

The doctor was the head of the department of Egyptian studies at the University of Texas and was the stereotype of the pointy-headed academic Bracken had complained about to Mr. Coleman.

He was a thin man in his fifties, tall with a neatly trimmed beard with bony hands at the end of arms that appeared too long for his body. He was dressed in a pair of tan cotton pants that looked not unlike the Dickie's work pants most West Texas farmers wore; but Jake knew this man had no first-hand experience with buying work clothes at Wal-Mart.

Completing the outfit was a long sleeve white shirt that was two sizes too big. It was easy to see the shirt had not seen a starched crease in years. A wide-brimmed straw hat and sunglasses like the ones Bracken wore were affixed to the man's head.

Dr. Kate Compton was one of the doctor's first graduate students. She was dressed this morning in jeans, work boots, a hat and button-up blue check shirt tucked into her jeans. She was not an unattractive woman but the rigors of spending so much time in the dry desert had taken their toll on her complexion. She was in her late thirties but had the energy of a much younger woman.

When she had first been introduced to Bracken, she had sized him up quickly as another rogue pilot and mentally dismissed him as just one more of the hired help.

To her annoyance, she found her assessment actually amused him and the fact that Bracken neither acknowledged her dislike of him nor cared one way or another about what she thought of him further compounded her frustration.

Unlike the other American men, she had met on these expeditions, Bracken had never made a pass at her and treated her with courtesy as if this were a bank in downtown Dallas in the sixties.

"But it's vital that Ms. Compton get some very important documents to Paris right away," he heard Dr. Walker say as he got within earshot.

"I didn't say she couldn't come with us," Platte replied, "I just said it wasn't my decision to make. I'm just the ground pounder here." Platte caught Bracken in his peripheral vision. "Ah, here is the man of the hour now." Leon turned to face Bracken as he spoke.

"Trouble?" Bracken asked, giving Leon a hard look.

On more than one occasion in his long association with Platte, he had found himself embroiled in a situation Leon had stirred up before he got on the scene. He had learned to be careful when Platte was pleading that he was a simple West Texas boy. But before Leon could answer the woman began speaking.

"This," Kate shot Leon a disgusted look, "cretin refuses to allow me to ride with you to Paris."

"That ain't so," Leon protested loudly.

"Which part," Bracken asked him, "the cretin part or the ride part?" Leon looked at his partner in mock dejection before answering.

"The ride part, of course," he said with a flash of white teeth. He seemed more than happy to lay claim to the other part of the disagreement.

"Now see here," the professor began in a pseudo tone of British nobility that all academics seemed to use when trying to make a forceful impression. Bracken turned his attention from Platte and on to the older man as he continued.

"Ms. Compton has information vital to this project that must be reviewed at the *Institute d'Etudes Politiques de Paris* as soon as possible. "

"Since I understand from your," the professor gave Platte the male version of the look he had just received from Kate, "assistant that the two of you are departing for Paris, I see no reason for you not to deny her passage on your plane."

Bracken rolled his eyes and couldn't help but wonder where this man acquired his sense of common courtesy and use of the English language. He spoke like they were about to embark on a weeks long cruise aboard a ship to Liverpool.

Platte had known Bracken long enough to realize his friend had very little patience when it came to these types of verbal exchanges. He knew any minute now, Bracken would reach his endurance for this particular art of the formal language. He didn't have long to wait. Even before the professor finished pleading his case Jake cut him off.

"Now, you see here, my good doctor," Bracken began in a cynical imitation of the professor's mannerisms. "I don't mind your assistant bummin' a ride with us. I'm even sure we have enough room on board to squeeze in one skinny female archeologist, but I don't much like anyone tellin' me what I have to do with, or who or what I can or cannot haul on my plane." Bracken emphasized the words 'on my plane'.

"You'd find us much more amiable if you stopped thinking that we're Uber drivers that you can have at the tap of your phone," he told the man, switching now to a forceful North Texas drawl.

"If y'all want a seat on the next flight outta here, you're gonna have to ask." Bracken finished by crossing his arms over his chest in a definitive act of defiance.

"Nicely, too," Leon mumbled.

The professor was used to bullying young wide-eyed graduate students who hung on his every word, but none of his previous experience gave him the slightest clue about how to deal with this tall middle-aged pilot, who seemed to bore a hole through you with his eyes. He just stood there, staring at Bracken unable to speak. His assistant finally came to his rescue.

"In that case, Mr. Bracken," she began in a timid voice hinting of female vulnerability, "would you mind allowing me to accompany the two of you to Paris? The doctor and I would be most grateful." She smiled at the two men in a most disarming way. It was all Bracken could do to keep from laughing out loud; it was quite an impressive performance.

"Since you put it that way ma'am," Jake said with a slight bow, "it would be our pleasure." He smiled at the woman as he turned and walked towards his tent.

Before Platte turned to do the same, he decided to extract a little revenge of his own.

"So, get packed and have your ass at the plane by 6:00 AM tomorrow morning or we're leaving without you." He started to follow his partner, thought better of what he had just said, and turned to deliver one final instruction.

"And pack light."

CHAPTER THREE

Valley of The Kings – Luxor Governorate, Egypt

If Leon was embarrassed by the fact Kate got to the plane before either he or Bracken arrived, it didn't show. Jake was surprised to find her, along with a single canvas bag and a well-worn backpack, standing in the shade of one of the wings, as he and Platte tumbled out of the back of a pickup truck in which they had bummed a ride to the airfield.

Jake walked past Kate, nodded a greeting and smiled, while he fished around in his pocket for the key to the plane.

Platte, on the other hand, decided to change tactics from their last encounter. He halted in front of Kate and gave her a large toothy grin. Before she even knew what he was doing, Platte had her bag in one hand and was leading her by the elbow towards the aircraft with the other hand.

He helped her into the plane, while Jake made his way into the cockpit. Leon stowed her bag, carefully and tied it down with elastic bungee cords. Her one bag handled, Leon showed her to the cockpit and pointed out a seat in front of what used to be the navigator's table for her to sit at.

She wondered if she was going to be required to perform some task for which she knew she was not trained. He read the question in her eyes, and pointed to the control panel between the pilot and co-pilot's seats.

"GPS," he told her.

"What's that?" She asked, thinking it was something she should know.

"Global Positioning Satellite," Bracken answered over his shoulder, as he studied a map.

"Navigators with stopwatches and those little circle drawing thingies..." Platte picked up from his pilot.

"Protractor," Bracken said in an informative tone, over the same shoulder, in Leon's direction this time, while still studying the map.

"Protractor," Leon confirmed and began again, "are a thing of the past. We use a transponder to triangulate our position using some 20-odd satellites in orbit over the earth. It can give us second-by-second location accurate to within a few feet. Much more accurate than drawing little circles on paper maps with those," Leon paused as Jake glanced up from the map and gave him a challenging look, "protractors."

Leon moved into the co-pilot's seat and buckled himself into the regulation three-point harness, then pulled a pair of aviator sunglasses out of his shirt pocket and fitted them on his face.

Jake picked up a 5 x 7 ring-bound set of plastic laminated cards sandwiched inside a hard cover held together with looping metal rings and handed it to Platte. Leon flipped it open and started reading aloud.

"Engine Run-Up Check-List" Platte read in an even voice void of his earlier lightheartedness.

"Ready," Bracken told him.

"Tailwheel?" Platte asked, grasping a grease pencil and positioning it over the first page.

"Locked," Bracken answered placing his hand on a lever between the two seats.

"Brakes?" Leon asked, marking a tickmark with the grease pencil by the appropriate item on the checklist.

"Set," came the reply after Bracken again touched the appropriate handle. Leon marked the laminated sheet again.

"Mixture levels?"

"Auto Rich," Jake said, pulling a knob on the control panel between them. The question and answer session continued for almost 15 minutes with Platte asking and Bracken checking the appropriate lever, switch, gauge, or breakers.

The process concluded with Leon closing the book as Bracken said "Clear right," Platte opened the window on his side of the plane and yelled back.

"Clear," he responded.

"Turning one." And with that, the plane shuddered and shook briefly, as the Pratt & Whitney Radial 1830 engine coughed to life.

The two men exchanged roles as soon as the first engine smoothed out to a steady idle. Jake stuck his head out of the left side of the plane, as Platte fired over the second engine.

When both engines were running and another checklist had been completed, Bracken eased off the brake, applied power to the engines and nudged the plane onto the short dirt-packed runway.

They taxied the entire length before turning the plane into the wind. Bracken scanned the instruments one more time, then pulled the control yoke all the way to his chest, and then pushed it forward as far as he could before returning it to a neutral position. Satisfied with this final check, he shoved both throttles to their forward stops.

The aged plane responded like an older, but still graceful runner jumping off the blocks and sprinting down the racecourse. About two-thirds of the way down the strip, Plate, who had been watching the ground speed, called " V2, Rotate"

Bracken pulled the yoke towards him, and the plane slowly lifted on a level horizon off the ground.

Before the plane had cleared the field, Platte flipped a three-inch lever, and Kate felt the airframe shudder as the landing gear folded up into places under each engine. Bracken brought the plane around 180 degrees and then began a slow but steady climb.

After fifteen minutes, Jake stopped the climb and leveled the plane out. Kate looked over the gauges until she found one that read Air Speed and Altimeter. The plane was traveling just around 150 miles per hour at about 10,000 feet above sea level. Jake turned and spoke to his partner.

"Take it," he said. Platte put both his hands on the control yoke.

"Co-pilot's airplane," he acknowledged. Jake pushed his seat back and reached into his coat pocket, withdrawing his pipe, battered tobacco pouch and lighter. He packed the bowl and lit it with long inward puffs that caused the flame to leap from the pipe with the increase in the oxygen flow.

"Phew!" cried Kate, waving her hand in front of her face. "Do you have to do that in here?" Bracken just smiled and scooted his seat back to the control yoke.

"Pilot's plane," he said taking the control wheel in his hands.

"Pilot has the airplane," Leon replied. Jake continued to puff on his pipe while looking out the windshield.

The day was clear and the sun that was just starting to rise was now streaming in through the right side of the co-pilot's window as the plane quickened their view of the dawn by increasing its angle on the horizon as it flowed the curve of the earth.

Bracken increased the flow of outside air, which reduced the amount of pipe smoke swirling in the cockpit to no more than he was puffing out of the pipe; whether out of courtesy or simply out of habit, Kate couldn't tell.

"How far is it from here to Paris?" She asked after looking at the needle of the airspeed indicator, rocking gently at 150 miles per hour. Bracken didn't answer but turned to Platte.

"A fine navigator you brought along," he said to his co-pilot.

"Me?" Leon asked in mock indignation. "I thought you hired her." With a grin, he turned in his seat.

"To Cairo, about 300 miles as the crow flies. From there to Paris, about 2000 miles again as the crow flies." Kate looked at her watch. It was just a little after 7:00 AM.

"How long will it take?" She asked again, looking at the airspeed indicator. To answer her Leon turned not to Kate but to Bracken.

"Dinner in Paris?" He asked.

"Isn't that what I promised you?" Bracken shot back, looking out his side of the cockpit to the ground below. Then Platte turned to answer the woman directly.

"Including our stop in Cairo," Leon said glancing at his watch, "eight hours tops."

"Eight hours?" She questioned. She glanced back at the airspeed indicator, which was still reading a steady 150 miles per hour.

She quickly added 300 and 2,000 in her head and then divided it by their current, and she supposed top, airspeed and came up with a number greater than eight. She looked back to Platte, who had been observing her with a sly smile, as she tried to do the math in her head.

"How do you expect to cover twenty-three hundred miles at 150 miles per hour in only eight hours?"

"An excellent question," Platte agreed. "I will inquire of the flight crew." He turned towards Bracken.

"How say you, oh winged one?" Bracken glanced over at Platte, already aware he was leading the woman down a prime rose path. Platte's eyes pleaded with him to along with the gag.

"Strong tailwinds," Bracken told him, and turned back to his pipe and the instrument panel.

"Our flight crew has informed me that our flying time will be reduced by strong tailwinds on the route," Platte told her in his best cabin crew manner.

Still not believing a word Platte said, but unable to come up with a more plausible explanation, she made a loud hurmf noise, fished a battered novel out of the backpack, and began to read. Platte moved back around to take up his position at the controls and grinned madly at Bracken.

"A fine navigator you brought along," Bracken repeated. Leon just shrugged, and pulled his cap down over his eyes for a short nap.

Kate did not become aware of the joke they had played at her expense until after they had landed at Cairo International and taxied to the private hangars at the end of the airfield.

In front of a hangar, bearing the Solaris Logo sat a small, eight-passenger, twin-engine Citation business jet painted in the Solaris colors with a ground crew standing by.

Once their DC3 was parked and chalked Bracken, Platte, and Kate with her luggage in tow, abandoned the DC3 for the smaller, but much faster jet.

Bracken spent a few minutes walking around the plane and talking to the ground crew, while Platte stowed their luggage and helped Kate into the passenger compartment.

Once Bracken was on board, the two men went through a similar but shorter checklist, started the engines, received taxi clearance, and rolled to the end of the runway.

"Cairo Tower," Bracken keyed into the throat microphone he had put on while they taxied. "This is Solaris Tango Alpha Charlie 149 requesting permission for Active 24R." There was a short pause before the reply came back in heavily Arabic-accented English over the cabin speakers.

"Solaris 149 your flight plan is cleared to Orly, Paris. Winds are at 260 at three knots, visibility is five miles at ten. At five thousand feet, turn left and take up a heading of 318 true north. You are cleared to 30. Notify Madrid Center on 1620 Megahertz upon reaching cruise. You are number one for take-off. Solaris 149, notify when rolling."

"Thank you, Cairo; Solaris 149 is rolling." And with that, Bracken turned the plane onto the active runway and pushed the throttles to their stops all in one motion. Kate felt the plane quickly gather speed down the runway.

Kate was angry and intended to express that to the two pilots, but thought it best to wait until they had managed to take off and smooth out higher up on the way to Paris.

While she waited, she looked out the window at the coastline of Egypt. As she looked out the port the early morning hour to ensure she arrived at the airfield before the two clowns flying the plane, caught up with her and she drifted off.

She woke with a start as the plane flared right before bouncing down on the end to the runway at Orly International Airport in Paris. As they taxied, Kate looked out the window at Paris' busy second metropolitan airport.

Both large and small planes alike danced the complex ballet of ground control, as they jockeyed for position and moved to and from the active runways.

Bracken guided their small jet to another hangar like the one in Cairo marked with Solari's logos, and shut the engines down. As Kate walked to the front of the plane, Platte moved in a stooping shuffle out through the cockpit door.

"Have a nice nap?" He asked her as he approached the door that opened to the outside world. She just glared at him in reply.

Platte turned from her grinning, and stood looking through the tiny porthole in the cabin door. The bang of someone's fist on the outside echoed through the cabin door, as Platte, in one fluid motion, popped the door open and swung it inside the passenger compartment of the plane.

"Too bad; not only did you miss the movie, but you missed the in-flight meal. And it's so seldom we have truffles and duck in cream sauce on Air Solaris."

Kate didn't retort, but grabbed her backpack and went down the stairs, which had extended from the plane when Platte opened the door. She almost knocked Bracken down in the process, as he emerged from the cockpit.

"What's with her?" Bracken asked his copilot in a tone that made it clear that he was positive whatever it was undoubtedly Platte's fault.

"I wouldn't swear to it, but I don't think she likes truffles." Bracken was about to open his mouth to say something but thought better of it.

A car transported the trio to the main terminal building where they quickly cleared French customs and passport control. From there, the three made their way through the ticketing area and down to the lower levels of the airport complex to the train station.

"What, no cab?" Kate asked Bracken, after he had sent Platte off to buy tickets for the next express to Paris. Bracken just laughed.

"Mr. Coleman has kittens when we expense €75 cab rides, especially since he knows the train station is right inside the airport."

"Who's Mr. Coleman?"

"My boss," Bracken told her nonchalantly as Platte rejoined the two. "All set?"

"Got'um," Leon answered, handing each a ticket. They navigated the turnstile and boarded their designated train. It silently left the station several minutes later gaining speed as the train exited the airport complex and moved west towards the city of Paris.

Kate had been to Paris several times, but had never ridden the trains, even though she was aware of how efficient and quick they were.   The day was a misty gray, and the sun was into its west path towards England.

A combination of lighting effects gave the suburbs of the city a muted and quiet look. She saw people and cars moving around, but none of the sounds penetrated the thickness of the interior. This impression was erased, forty-five minutes later, after they had gotten off the train, and she followed Platte, who was in turn following Bracken, up the stairs and out of the underground train station.

The cacophony of the traffic on the street and the voices of the crowds of people moving down the wide walkway assaulted her the moment they emerged into the open air. She turned to ask where they were going, but stopped as she caught sight of the Eiffel Tower a mere six blocks away.

She stood transfixed looking at the impressive structure that Gustoff Eiffel had built for the 1897 World's Fair. In her earlier trips to the French capital, she had seen the Eiffel Tower, but from a distance. She was always too busy to take the time needed to play tourist and to look at it from a closer vantage point.

When she finally caught herself and looked around, she noticed Platte, and her canvas bag, which he was faithfully carrying along with his own backpack of a suitcase, were several hundred yards ahead of her and moving towards the tower.

She had almost caught up with him, when he turned down Rue de la Suffern. When she followed suit, she finally had a clue where the two men were heading: a large semi-curved building displaying the Hilton logo. Bracken was already in the process of registering when she entered the lobby.

Her annoyance with the pair returned when she realized that she had not been consulted about where they were going to stay for the night, and she intended to tell Bracken so when he finished with his breezy and all-too-lighthearted conversation with the young woman behind the desk.

Similar to Bracken's earlier comments about his boss' aversion to expensive cab rides, she was sure the University of Texas, Dallas would frown on her attempts to expense a night's stay at a four-star Parisian hotel. But once again, this most annoying man had preempted her protest.

When he stepped away from the desk, leaving the clerk smiling, he handed her a credit card style room key.

"What's this?" she asked after a momentary pause. Bracken gave her the same look he had given Platte when he had questioned his choice of navigators.

"It's a room key, I think," he said taking it back from her and turning it over in his hand. He gave it back to her. "Yep, that's what it is."

"I can't afford to stay here," she protested.

"Well, we can't afford to be chasing you around all over Paris because you feel the need to save a few shekels on accommodations."

"Look here," she said, her emotions finally coming to her rescue. "I'm perfectly capable of taking care of myself. I have things I need to do here that do not include you and your plans for carousing away the evening in Paris."

"Bracken never carouses," Platte joining the conversation. "He likes eating too much. If you want to carouse, you should stick with me. I am persona non grata in several whole districts of the city." Bracken cut him off.

"No one's going carousing, least of all you," he said to Platte sternly. "Remember what happened last time at the Lido?"

"That was a simple misunderstanding," Platte said with a wry grin. "I was just trying to guess the girl's weight," Platte would have continued his self-defense, but once more Bracken stepped on his diatribe.

"Look, Ms. Compton," Bracken said, turning his attention back to Kate. "You don't have to pay for the room tonight. You are a guest of Solaris for the evening. I don't think Leon and I have not been as nice to you as we could have been. I would like to make it up to you, and invite you to join us for dinner. I can promise you a wonderful meal, and we won't embarrass you." He flashed her a sincere smile. "I'll even make Leon use silverware."

She started to refuse and tell him to find someone else to take to dinner; but something in his eyes and the openness of his face convinced her that he was truly trying to be nice. Before she could stop herself, she heard her own voice agreeing to the arrangement.

They formed a plan to meet in the bar at seven, before striking out for dinner. Bracken told her which room was hers, and they boarded the elevator together. Her floor was first stop and as the doors closed behind her, she heard Platte asking if not embarrassing Kate meant he still could eat his peas with a knife and honey.

CHAPTER FOUR

15th District – Paris, France

After a thirty-minute nap, a long hot shower and a change of clothes, Platte walked into the bar to find Kate had once more beaten him to the prearranged place. He pulled the chair out from under the small table and grabbed a handful of peanuts in all one motion.

"Where's your sidekick?" She asked, as he tried to get the bartender's attention.

"I'm not sure you could ever call Jake Bracken anyone's sidekick," he said, after swallowing the peanuts. "But to answer your question, the last I saw of him, he was in the middle of a rather heated discussion with our Solaris office in Dallas. He said he'd be running a little late and asked me to keep you company until he got here."

"And so," Kate began, taking a sip from her half empty glass of wine, "like the rest of us, you do what Mr. Bracken says without question, is that it?"

A wounded expression crossed Platte's and he sat looking down at for several long minutes before answering.

"Dr. Compton," he began, emphasizing her title, "I am sure you're really good at what you do; but I gotta tell you, I think you've been hanging around the dead too long; it's warped your perception of the livin'."

"How is that?" She countered preparing to be angry.

"Well ma'am," he continued again, slipping into a more pronounced West Texas drawl. "It's like this. I've been watchin' you spar with Jake ever since we arrived at the dig site. You can't decide if he's a condescending Texas male chauvinist or some playboy fly-boy who's just looking for a good time. The fact that he has exhibited neither tendency has just about driven you nuts."

Kate tried to hide her astonishment that this stranger had read her thoughts so accurately just by observing her actions. She started to retort but could not get the words out before Platte continued.

"You're right about one thing though," he continued, as the waiter finally approached their table. "I will gladly do whatever Bracken says." While the waiter took Platte's order it gave Kate time to reorganize her thoughts.

"Why is that?" she asked, as the waiter departed.

"For two very good reasons," he said turning his attention back to her. "First he's usually, ninety-nine-point nine percent right and second, because he honest to God saved my hide on more than one occasion; but the first one was enough for me to pledge my friendship to him for the rest of my life."

"You've got to be kidding?" she asked him leaning into the table.

"No, ma'am. Jake Bracken pulled momma Platte's baby boy right out of the jaws of death." He glanced around before continuing his story, and Kate got the distinct feeling that he was checking to be sure that Bracken wasn't within earshot.

"I was on a job for Solaris down in Columbia," he continued once he confirmed that no one was listening. There's a ton of light sweet crude all over the place down there. The only thing Columbia's got more of than oil is rebels and drug dealers. Most days, you can find the same guys holding down both jobs at the same time.

"Jake was living in Columbia and flying as an independent contractor after, what was whispered in the bars around the airport, a rather colorful career in the Air Force; making good money at it too by all accounts." He paused for a moment as the waiter appeared with their drinks and took a long sip from the wine glass before taking up his tale anew.

"Anyway, one day I'm working about 10 miles north of this wide spot in the dirt road known as Turbo. It's about a hundred miles from the Panamanian border and smack dab in the middle of the Columbian superhighway between Panama's banks and Columbia's drug fields.

"This particular day, my team and I got caught in an all-out shooting war between the drug dealer/rebels and the Columbian Army. One of my guys got killed in the first exchange, and I took a round through my leg that shattered the bone into about a million pieces."

"One of the other guys is on the radio screaming to Jake to come and get us. And do you know what he did?"

"No," Kate avowed caught up in Platte's story.

"By God, he came to get us. A full-scale firefight raging around us, and this guy sets the Bell Ranger down within 50 feet of me, carries me to the helicopter, and takes off while they're shooting at each other and us.

"Just as we get airborne, someone's machine gun took out all the oil lines in the helicopter. We're only about 200 feet up and a mile away before the panel lights up red with every caution and warning light known to man."

"Bracken had to put the thing down in the jungle a good five miles out of Turbo, but he managed to do it without hurting anyone any more than they already were, or so we thought at the time."

"Then, the guy proceeds to carry me five miles through the jungles of Columbia to a little bar on the outskirts of town.

He called Solaris and told them where we were and asked them to kindly come and get us. By the time Solaris' security gets there all four of us are drunk on our ass. When I woke up the next day in the hospital, I couldn't decide which hurt worse, my bullet-induced broken leg or my Bracken-induced hangover."

Kate sat back and studied him to make sure this was not just another guy inventing a tale as a practical joke at her expense. She was surprised to see Platte attempt to remove something from his eye that wasn't there; there was no doubt this man was telling her the whole truth and nothing but the truth.

"What happened to him?" She asked, meaning Bracken.

"I was told, although you will never get it out of Jake, that he took my team and me to the hospital, where he collapsed from a round, he had taken while evacin' us out of the jungle. The guy almost bled to death, and never said a word to anyone about it." Platte told her before turning back to his drink.

"Kinda macho, isn't he?" She could tell by the fire that immediately blazed in Platte's eyes that she had asked, if not the wrong thing, at least in the wrong way. She decided to quickly change the subject.

"How did he end up at Solaris?" She wanted to know. Leon pondered for a moment before answering her. She knew instinctively that he wasn't thinking about what to say, but whether he should bother answering at all.

"When Mr. Coleman, who is now President and CEO of Solaris, heard about what Bracken did to get us out of harm's way, he flew to Columbia, and right on the spot, offered Jake a job," Platte informed her curtly.

"So, he got his job at Solaris as a reward for pulling you guys out of the firefight?" She asked. Leon thought he detected a slight rebuke in her question. Platte looked at her and continued.

"Nope, Jake turned him down flat. Twice, as the story goes."

"So how did he end up at Solaris?" She repeated as her prejudgment of the pilot was shot down once again.

"About six months after we got back to Texas, ol' Jake shows up at Puzzle Palace says he's looking for a grubstake," Platte answered.

"Puzzle Palace?" She inquired.

"Bracken's *nom de plume* for Solaris' headquarters in Dallas.

"So, he got a job and now he's a company pilot." She said once again attempting to find fault with Bracken and his motives.

"You know, you are one hardhearted woman," Platte declared as he leaned back in his chair. "You have any idea what a pilot for an oil company does?" Kate shook her head.
"Well, let me tell you. Most of the time, he's flying in and out of airstrips that are too short and narrow and don't exist on any map."

"Frequently, you're flying into places that are hostile because the environment is too cold, too hot, or too wet, or because one of the local tribes/warlords/or Armies of the day is at war with one another or at war with Solaris. Trust me, it ain't like doing the Dallas – Houston run for Southwest Airlines."

Both of them picked up their drinks again, as they mulled over what Platte had just said. Platte drained his glass and signaled the passing, and uninterested waiter, for another round.

"I'll tell you something else," he said when he'd finished with the waiter. "Bracken is more than just a pilot."

"Oh?" Kate asked. "What else is he?" She wanted to know. This earned her another glaring rebuke from Platte, who finally just shook his head before answering.

"I'm not sure how to put it into words, but for some reason, Mr. Coleman sends Bracken whenever he's not comfortable with what's happening where Solaris has a project in place."

"Jake's a trouble-shooter. Not in the traditional Ivy League sorta way, most of these young hotshots today think of troubleshooting, showing up with a laptop and a suit." He said almost spitting out the words in obvious disgust.

"When Solaris has trouble on a project, Mr. Coleman sends Bracken out on some silly errand for a few days. Bracken, who is a curious sorta fellow, as long as he's awake, wanders around asking questions and looking things over.

The next thing you know, a couple of guys ain't working there no more and things seem to get back to normal, which for Solaris means pumping barrels of oil out of a well. As far as I know, he's not trained in any part of an oil company's operations, but he's got Mr. Coleman's trust and he get things done."

He deliberated for a moment before continuing. "I doubt Jake even knows what he's really doing there."

As if on cue, Jake Bracken strolled into the bar in an easy loping stride that said as much to Kate about him as anything Platte had just said.

He was dressed in a gray suit and black mock turtleneck pullover. His hair showed the effects of a recent encounter with a comb but, did not appear to have been brought into submission. He was smiling warmly and openly.

It occurred to Kate, that as far as she could recall, in the three weeks or so that she had known him he was either smiling that smile or trying to hide it when he talked to you.

He took in the whole room at a glance. It was something that he did instinctively. Kate knew that he had spotted them right away, but he took his time making his way to the table.

In spite of the fact, the French are generally reserved and private people; Jake smiled and greeted the waiter and several people around the bar in his open Texas manner.

Although no one returned his greeting and in a couple of instances people took offense to his American manners, it did not seem to bother him in the least. He was determined to be friendly, regardless of the customs of the country. Jake was Jake, and that was that. For some reason, Kate liked that about him; then immediately hated herself for it.

What was it about this guy that both attracted her and repelled her at the same time? The things Leon just told her had somewhat changed her opinion of the man, but at the same time, she couldn't overcome her earlier, and now seemingly unfounded assessment, of this man.

She had struggled for so long to make it in her own world with nothing but her wits and accomplishments. She had known women who left studies and promising careers to "settle down and raise a family" with men just like Jake Bracken. She had advised those same women about how stupid and senseless it was to get sucked into that kind of security when they could easily make it on their own.

While she was nowhere close to wanting to trade in her degree for an apron, she was annoyed that, without even trying, this man was getting to her, and as he approached the table, for the life of her, she couldn't figure out why.

"I hope you've behaved yourself," Bracken said to Platte.

"I have a witness" Platte replied, pointing to Kate.

"Oh yeah," Kate began, "he's has been filling me in on the adventures of…" She stopped short when she felt Platte's foot pressing down on her foot under the table.

It was now painfully obvious to her that Platte didn't want Bracken to know what he had just told her. She surrendered to the mild pain and the entreaty in Leon's eyes and salvaged her reply, "…drilling for oil, in a place like Egypt." Bracken looked at Platte who just smiled. He didn't believe her but had no clue what Platte had been telling her.

Jake sat down at their table, while Leon motioned for the waiter, who was busy ignoring the threesome. When he finally arrived, Jake smiled openly at him, which seemed only to deepen the scowl on his face and betray his dislike for Americans.

"I believe we will leave for dinner soon, and with that in mind," Jake said, "we should have an aperitif." He turned to the waiter and held up two fingers and his thumb to indicate the number three, in the European counting style. "Three Kir Royale, please."

"What's that?" Kate asked, wondering why Jake ordering for her did not bother her.

"It is a combination of champagne and black liquor," he said. "You can make it with white wine, but then it is called simply a Kir."

The waiter returned quickly, more motivated by a desire to get these Americans filled up and, on their way, than from a desire to provide good service. When everyone had a glass, Jake lifted his in a toast to the table.

"Here's to good times and good food," he said with a flourish.

"What, no good liquor and good women?" Leon asked in mock disenchantment. Jake offered him what could only be described as a weary look. "OK, OK how about just good liquor and bad women? They're more fun anyway." Spontaneously, Kate reentered the conversation.

"Which," she wanted to know, "good liquor or bad women?"

"Well," he said downing his drink, "at this point in the evening, I'm willing to settle for either one."

They quickly finished their drinks, walked out of the hotel bar, and onto the street separating the hotel from the Eiffel Tower. Moving down the wide and tree-lined sidewalk, it was obvious that the three of them were acquaintances, but not friends. They moved and talked in a sociable manner but did not move close to each other as friends would.

Hindered by the hasty intake of the drink she was just now beginning to wonder what kind of place these two were taking her to. She was sure it was either someplace cheap and tawdry, so as to embarrass her, or someplace on the other end of the spectrum, expensive and outlandish, anticipating the same effect. They had gone about a mile, when Leon waived to a waiter standing on the sidewalk in front of a medium-sized neighborhood restaurant.

The waiter recognized both men and motioned them to a table on the sidewalk. To Kate's utter annoyance, Bracken insisted on holding her chair out for her. When she was seated, she looked at Platte who was struggling to stifle a grin and was doing so by shaking his head in an amused fashion.

When the waiter returned, he was armed with menus for the group. After passing them out, the waiter said something to Leon in French. She was about to offer her assistance, but before she could, she heard, in a voice that sounded very much like Platte's responding to the waiter in flawless French. Leon then engaged the waiter in a fast-flowing conversation concerning the specials of the night.

The young man asked if they would like something to drink. Without looking at the menu, Leon ordered, a bottle of white wine, and sent the waiter off on his errand, with a friendly sweep of his hand. Sensing Kate's surprise at his command of the local language, he looked at her and winked.

"Look, dear, we've all got our little secrets." He laughed and turned his attention towards the gathering at the bar inside. The wine was brought, and Leon went through the time-honored ritual of inspecting the cork, swirling the liquid in the glass, and the tasting of a small sample of the vintage.

Once he was satisfied that it was indeed the fruit of the grapes of Loire Valley, as opposed to common vinegar, the waiter poured a liberal round into everyone's glass before retreating. They drank in silence while inspecting the menu.

When their glasses were almost empty, the young waiter reappeared to pour another round for them and transcribe their selections for dinner. Before he left, Leon ordered another bottle of wine.

They engaged in small talk about where they lived and what they did. Leon's stories were filled with graphic Technicolor details that illustrated what he was talking about.

When Jake was asked about one aspect or another of his life, past, or present, he would mumble a general comment and then try to goad Leon once more.

Kate found she had an uncontrollable need to impress her host with tales of her travels and adventures. When it finally dawned on her that she was checking to see how Jake was responding to her stories, she was exasperated and asked Leon for directions to the lady's room.

"What the hell am I doing?" She asked her reflection in the mirror. "What do I care what this flyboy thinks?" She knew that she didn't sound very convincing as the echo in the room returned her words to her ears. She did the best she could to collect her thoughts and returned to the table where she found both dinner and another full glass of wine waiting for her.

Jake didn't realize how hungry he was until he got a whiff of the plate placed in front of him. Despite what Leon had joked about the in-flight meal, in actually their lunch had been sandwiches and lukewarm coffee.

It had been a long day already, and he was tired and hungry. Although flying the DC3 required all of his skill and attention, it was a short flight and the weather had not posed much of a challenge. The Citation, he mused, flew itself for all intents and purposes.

The onboard computer-controlled autopilot could actually land the plane if necessary, but international law and Bracken's own preferences dictated that the pilot control the plane while landing, which he did. He wondered if he was just getting too old for his unusual lifestyle, but ego, pride, fear or a combination of all three demanded that he reject that answer from the list of things that he was willing to consider as the cause of his weariness.

Dinner concluded with the melodic accompaniment of the traffic on the street and the occasional gusts of laughter that floated from around the bar to the outside dining tables. When they declared themselves full and laid their silverware aside, Leon excused himself and entered the restaurant.

Kate thought that he was just going to the men's room, but when she looked through the window, she saw he had joined the group leaning on the bar. She noticed he was telling the barmaid something, and from the look on her face, it was something that both embarrassed and pleased her. She nodded towards the window.

"It seems you've lost your boy." Kate said. Bracken looked in, spotted Leon, and turned back to her with a tired smile.

"Well, for starters, I doubt he would like it if you called him my boy to his face. He may look like some West Texas bumpkin in the big city for the state fair, but as you already deduced on your own, Leon is anything but a simple West Texas boy, and certainly nobody's fool." Jake told her while fishing his pipe out of the pocket. Kate realized for the second time in as many hours that she had been warned about the pitfalls of misjudging either of these two.

"You know that he thinks you hung the moon, don't you?" She questioned. Jake didn't immediately reply. He looked into the bar and slowly lit the pipe with a match from a book on the table.

"He has this misguided perception that he owes me for saving his life." He hid his face behind a cloud of smoke as he spoke.

"From what he tells me I'm convinced that he does." As the smoke screen dispersed, she looked directly into his face. What she saw was genuine embarrassment.

"Well," Jake said, remaining focused on his pipe, "it was a long time ago, and as he might have pointed out to you lots of people were shooting at us. It's pretty easy to get confused in a situation like that." He replaced the pipe into his mouth and pulled on it with slow delight before picking up the conversation.

"Besides," Jake smiled around the pipe stem, "stories always get more gruesome every time Leon tells them." He pulled the pipe out of his mouth and looked at Kate.

"Tell me something," Jake asked motioning towards her with his hand, "how in the world did you end up in the desert, with that skinny professor from Dallas, sifting through the sand in the Valley of the Kings?"

"Oh," she said heaving a sigh and running her hand through her hair, "that's a long story."

"I think we have the time." He said nodding towards the window. She looked to see that the barmaid had come from behind the bar and joined Leon at a small table. Kate smiled.

"I was full of missionary zeal," she began in response to his question. "I graduated from college armed with a Ph.D. in Ancient Studies and expected the world to come to my feet begging for the knowledge I had to impart. What I discovered was the world at large wasn't interested in a well-educated turned-out Doctor of Ancient Studies.

"I was nearly out of money when I found out Dr. Walker, who had been one of my undergrad professors, was going to head up a dig in the Valley of the Kings, and he needed an assistant. I applied, got the job and I've been there ever since. That was in the early 1990s, the rest is more recent history."

Jake smiled at her attempt at humor. He could sense bitterness in her voice, but he wasn't sure if it came from the fact, she found that her Doctorate didn't translate well into big money jobs, or the fact that society as a whole didn't place much value in her chosen life's work.

"In fact," she continued, "where we're working now is more of less the same spot we were working back then. Oh my, that was almost 20 years ago," she said in shock as she added up the years in her head.

Over the next hour the second bottle of wine was drained and turned into a third that met the same fate as the first two. To her amazement Bracken turned out to be a good listener.

The wine helped to free her tongue, and she found herself telling Bracken not only about the trials and tribulations of working around the over-educated living and the long-dead royalty of Egypt, but also about other parts of her life.

She told him about growing up middle class in the Midwest. Without thinking she also told him of early loves and broken hearts were interwoven with stories about archeological digs in the middle of hostile foreign countries.

She didn't intend to tell him so much, and in fact, as she heard stories of her own life coming out of her own mouth. She longed to cut it off but found she couldn't.

Bracken listened with interest to everything she had to say and showed an equal interest in both her professional and personal life. He asked her questions out of a genuine curiosity in order to round out his understanding of what she was saying.

Before she knew it, the waiter approached Jake and informed him that it was, what Kate assumed to be, the French version of the last call, and asked him if he needed anything else from the bar or the kitchen. Jake assured him they were perfectly fine. After the waiter retreated, he stood and prepared to leave.

"It seems we have outlasted the wait staff." Kate shot him a quizzical glance and he translated for her. "They're closing."

"Oh", she said. As Jake stood, he laid an assortment of Euro bills on the table. The waiter returned, wished them a good evening, and thanked them for coming.

Jake pressed a folded bill into the waiter's hand and in halting, French told him it was, *"pour quelque chose à boire,",* for something to drink, which is the French equivalent of a tip.

When Kate finally stood up the combined effects of her Kir Royale and her share of the three bottles of wine hit her like a ton of bricks. She found that, much like her flight in Bracken's plane earlier that day, she was seeking the artificial horizon to make sure she was standing on level ground. Bracken noticed her distress and moved quickly towards her.

"You know," he said as he slid his arm smoothly under hers for support, "you need to train for that kinda rapid takeoff." She wanted to tell him to leave her alone but, very quickly realized that she would need help to walk back to the hotel.

They were almost halfway to the hotel before she remembered Platte.

"Where's your buddy?" She asked.

"Well despite the fact that I personally think Leon needs a fulltime keeper, he really can manage to get home on his own," he replied with a smiled.

"Those sorry bastards," she thought to herself. *"they arranged this. I wonder what the cue was for Platte to disappear."* She made a vain attempt to pull away from Bracken and succeeded to a point. As she did, she

realized that she could not be trusted to support her own weight up and navigate the lamplight Paris streets.

"Pity the poor sailors at sea on a night like this," Bracken chuckled, as she once more tightened her grip on his arm.

By the time they arrived at the hotel, the cool air and the walk had helped to clear some of the cobwebs out of her head.

"I wonder when he is going to make his move? So far, he has walked me here like a gentleman. He hasn't said anything that could even be remotely construed as inappropriate. Maybe he thinks if he takes it slow and just tries to kiss me goodnight, I'll want more? So, what is he up too?" It wasn't until the elevator ride up to the 9th floor that she figured it out.

"He's going to invite himself in for a nightcap, or something like that. He thinks his charm and mild-mannered ways have put me off my guard. Well, I got news for him!"

She was still contemplating all this by the time they reached to the door to her room. Jake released her arm and stepped back, while she fumbled the keycard out of her purse and inserted it into the electronic lock. The door clicked and flashed her a green light.

"I'll just step inside a little, quickly tell him good night, and close the door. And she did just that. As she opened the door and stepped inside, she braced herself to face Jake.

"I had a wonderful time tonight. I'd invite you in for a drink, but...." she began to say as she turned around, but found she was talking not to Jake but to the door of the room across the hall.

She heard whistling and followed the sound with her head, only to spot the man she'd assumed had dishonorable designs on her, was already halfway down the hallway to the elevator bank.

She stared after him for several moments before realizing that Jake Bracken had intended nothing more than to see her safely to her door. She blinked once more before ducking into the room and slamming the door.

She stood there for a long moment trying to comprehend why she was so disconcerted. Was it because she still suspected him of wanting something from her? Or was she offended because he didn't? She clenched both her hands into a fist, and in utter frustration, slapped them down onto her legs.   The process of doing this forced the room key out of her hand and she dropped it onto the floor in front of her.

She seldom swore, but either the fact that she'd had too much to drink or that she was still mad at Jake and could blame him, empowered her to utter curses in Arabic that day workers on dig site had taught her over the years.

She was now further annoyed because of the fact the room was dark, and she had to bend over to locate the key in order to turn on the lights. As she did so, two things happened simultaneously.

First, she heard and felt the movement of the air as something passed over her head and made a "whooshing" sound. Second, instead of the door key, what she found instead was a pair of shoes that were facing in the wrong direction to allow them to be the ones on her feet. They were also men's shoes she noted with some detachment.

Just at that moment a hand grabbed her hair and yanked her upright. Kate's reflex took control and she let out a blood-curdling scream that filled the room and traveled down the hall.

In the next instant, she felt an arm snake around her neck and felt a hand moving to cover her mouth as she continued to scream. When she felt the flesh of her attacker's hand cover her mouth, she bit down hard and was rewarded by a loud curse and a painful blow to the back of her head.

The agony from the blow immediately turn the room a milky white, which tunneled her vision into a narrow cone in front of her. She knew she was losing consciousness but, was unable to prevent it, as her vision continued to narrow to a speck in front of her.

Just as she was about to forsake her connection to the room around her, she sensed the arm loosening from her neck, and immediately after heard the loud crash of splitting wood.

Light from the hallway now flooded her room. As she regained some limited vision and saw the outline of her attacker move to face Jake, who was now standing in the splintered doorframe. The door itself was hanging off to one side, clinging to the hinges in a feeble attempt to stay connected to the doorjamb.

Kate could also see that her attacker was wielding a large knife in his hand. She reasoned that it was the knife that she heard in the whoosh that went over her head.

The man with the knife lunged at Jake from an off-balanced stance that took Bracken by surprise, so he didn't have a chance to fully shield his body from the thrust of the blade.

The blade caught him on the forearm, slicing a cut through his jacket and shirt, and then into his arm. Jake grunted, and jerked his arm away from the knife. The assailant then shifted into a position indicating he intended to make another pass at Bracken with the blade.

His stance and position implied that Jake was afraid to get hurt anymore. But there was enough light for Kate to see that the look in Jake's eyes did not match the message he was sending with his body.

The attacker gauged Jake's possible reaction smirked, and then lunged at him with the knife. At the last possible moment, before the blade again connected with his body, Jake pitched sideways with a skill and grace that surprised both the assailant and Kate; Jake let the man's momentum carry him out towards the hallway beyond the shattered door.

But, instead of reaching for the knife, Jake brought his hands up and grabbed the man's head tightly between his palms. Using his forward motion as a fulcrum Jake twisted the whole head sharply toward the left.

Kate heard the sickening sound of snapping bones, and the attacker dropped as if he had been poleaxed. He twitched once, and then lay motionless with his head at an unnatural angle, halfway in and halfway out of her room. A small trickle of blood ran from his nose.

The reality she had just seen, and what had almost happened to her physically overwhelmed her, and she knew she was fainting as she heard Jakes voice calling.

"Are you alright?" He asked as he faded from her view.

CHAPTER FIVE

15th District – Paris, France

Kate was walking in a field full of bright, yellow flowers with a black center. At first she was amazed because, ordinarily being surrounded by this much pollen, triggered a sneezing fit. She was so delighted to be outside in the sun and in the field of flowers; she stopped and bent over to inhale the sweet fragrance. But the closer she got, the more alarmed she became, because the odor emanating from the flowers was not sweet and faint, but instead, it was pungent and overpowering.

Instead it reminded her of a cleaning chemical. The smell was vaguely familiar, and she struggled in her mind to remember what it was. It finally dawned on her:

Ammonia

Instantly the vision vanished and was replaced with a view of the ceiling in her hotel room and a twenty-something French EMT, in a white smock, holding an ammonia capsule under her nose. She blinked at the transition and tried to sit up.

"Mademoiselle, Comment vous appelez-vous?" The white-smocked man inquired.

"What?" She asked.

"Comment vous appelez-vous?" He repeated, while taking her wrist and looking at his watch. Without waiting for her to respond, he released her wrist, removed a small penlight from his pocket, and shined it into her eyes.

"Comment tu te sens maintenant? Quel est votre nom?" As her thought process slowly cleared, she

realized that this young medic was asking, how she felt and her name.

The realization that her brain could finally understand what he was asking prompted her to remember that she also spoke French and answered him.

"*Je vais très bien, merci. Je m'appelle Dr. Compton, "* she said sitting up fully while assuring the young man she felt fine, and that her name was Dr. Compton, thanking him for his concern.

In actuality, she still felt a little fuzzy around the edges, but it was easier to assure the nice young man that she was feeling better than it was to accurately translate her questionable condition into French.

A flash of light diverted her attention from the medic to the doorway of her hotel room, where a police photographer was taking pictures of her assailant. He was still where he fell, with his head in an unnatural position. Her memory of her attack rushed into her head, including the sound of snapping bones and she twisted around to find Jake Bracken.

When she finally located him, he was half-sitting, half- leaning on the dresser while another EMT sutured through the gash on his forearm. She then swung her attention again back to the man who had attacked her and noticed the double-edged knife laying not far from his open hand.

The white-smocked medic working on Jake's arm, completed his sutures, and stepped to the side to retrieve something from his medical kit. The space in front of Jake now free, he took three long strides and bent down to Kate, keeping his arm level as he did so.

"How are you feeling?" He asked, brushing her cheek with a kiss. His actions so startled her that she didn't pull away. Jake moved his mouth from her cheek towards her ear and dropped his voice.

"It would probably good idea if you don't say much about this right now. I have no idea what the French laws are, but it would be best to say as little as possible to anyone right now." He surreptitiously glanced around to see if anyone had heard him, then he looked back at Kate. He could what she was thinking by the look in her eyes.

"I'm not asking you to lie," he told her still in a whisper, "just don't say any more then you have to, just now." She looked past him at her assailant in the doorway once again.

"Is he dead?" she asked, knowing full well that he was.

"Yes," Bracken said simply.

"But, but…," she stammered, "you killed him."

"Yes, I did," Bracken, breathed in a soft tone. His voice was devoid of any emotion. She looked closely into his eyes; if there was remorse in them for taking another man's life it didn't show.

For some unexplainable reason, Kate was convinced at that moment this was not the first time Jake Bracken had knowingly and intentionally killed someone. She started to say something else to him, but at that moment Leon made his way into the room and disrupted her train of thought.

Trailing behind Leon came a thin man wearing a suit, white shirt, and a dark blue tie. The police photographer sprang to his feet into a stance of attention and nodded towards the man in the suit, who then addressed another uniformed policeman also standing respectfully at attention.

There was a brief exchange between the two after which the policeman nodded to Jake and Kate.

"You alright?" Leon asked Bracken, as he stood up while gingerly flexing the fingers on his damaged arm.

"No," he said, waving his arm, "but, I will mend." He glanced questionably at the suited man who had followed Leon into the room.

"Head cop," Leon said under his breath, "we rode up in the elevator together." Kate knew that Leon wanted to say more, but he was interrupted by the medic who had been working on Jake's arm, who addressed the pair in rapid-fire French. Leon turned to him, responded in kind, and then turned back to Jake.

"The gentleman was wondering if you would allow him to finish bandaging your arm." Bracken cocked his head towards Leon.

"Admittedly," Bracken began, "I know next to nothing of the French language, but I suspect that, your translation, while capturing the basics of what the good corpsman just said, your exact translation was not completely accurate." Leon chuckled.

"Well, I will confess to a rather loose interpretation, while still capturing the spirit of his words. What he actually said was that if you don't get back over there and let him finish bandaging your arm, he was leaving, and hoped your arm turns black, rots, and falls off."

Jake smiled and acknowledged Platte's revised translation, then rose and returned to the medic who had sutured his arm. Using his good arm, he made a sweeping bow and spoke to the EMT.

"*Pardon*," he said, in West-Texas-accented French. The EMT just made a sour face and began wrapping Jake's arm in bandages.

Before Jake's arm was completely bandaged Leon had helped Kate to her feet. Jake, Leon, and Kate clustered together as far from the door and dead body as they could get.

They said nothing to each other as they observed the photographer snap his final pictures of the crime scene. With the photos finished, two uniformed policemen placed the corpse into a thick black plastic body bag.

The man Platte had identified as the head cop walked towards the three Americans, holding their passports in his hand. He pulled up short of them by a few feet, opened one of the passports, and flipped through the pages.

"Monsieur Bracken?" He asked, his head looking down at the document. "I see you and your friends are very well traveled," he said, nodding to one of the passports.

"However, I must wonder what is it with you Americans and your blood lust? Along with your pointless and cultureless adventure movies, why must you also export your violence to my country and my city?" He raised his head now and stared straight at Jake.

"Are you the lone cowboy who must engage in battle with his bare hands?" He challenged. Leon noticed the slight set come into Bracken's jaw as he returned the Frenchman's gaze. Jake stared for what seemed like a long time. Without moving his eyes or giving any quarter Jake spoke.

"As a general rule, I commit murder with my trusty six-shooter, and rarely, if ever, when I am not wearing my cowboy boots. But, seeing as this being Paris and all, the great city of lights, I try to make certain allowances for local customs," Jake answered coldly his eyes still locked with the suited Frenchman's.

"If you're trying to piss me off, to get me to say something careless, we can stop wasting each other's time. I will call my Embassy. Then you can interrogate us in a few days, after your bureaucrats, spend days with our bureaucrats, wading through all the proper diplomatic protocols." Bracken said, keeping his voice even and conversational, but with a slight edge to it.

"However," he resumed, "if you'll drop the stupid cop games, I'll forget the Embassy and tell you probably what you   want to know about what happened here tonight," he concluded nodding toward the door where the bagged body was being loaded onto a gurney.

The Frenchman shot Jake and icy stare, sizing him up for a moment longer, and came to a decision that he signaled with a slight shrug, and a noticeable relaxing of his shoulders.

"Jean Michael," the man said extending his hand. "*Préfecture de police de Paris Homocide* for the fifteenth district," he said in heavily French-accented English. Jake took the man's proffered.

"Jake Bracken, Solaris Oil Company, Dallas, Texas," he said shaking the inspector's hand. "This is Leon Platte also of Solaris and Dallas, and this is Dr. Compton, an educator from the University in Dallas, Texas." Handshakes were exchanged between all around.
"Homicide?" Kate asked.

"*Qui, mademoiselle,*" he replied, "you cannot deny that this man is very much dead, and that your friend Monsieur Bracken, killed him. I do not suppose we can judge this an accident, no?" He asked looking at Jake.

"Do any of you know who this man was?" Jean Michael asked. In one-way or another, they all indicated they did not. He then turned to Kate.

"Please to tell me, mademoiselle, what happened to you?" While the question was polite and spoken with softness Kate knew it was not a request and she had no choice but to answer.

She began slowly, her narrative gaining speed as it progressed up to the point where Jake crashed into the room. The inspector studied Kate as she answered listening, not only to what she said, but how she said it and observing her body language as she spoke.

"Had you seen the man lurking around the lobby, the hallway, or maybe in the bar? She shook her head no.

"Did he touch you in a manner that was sexual?" Kate's eyes widened at the question. "I am sorry, mademoiselle, but the question must be asked. He did not touch you, in any way to indicate that he had an interest in you physically?" Kate again shook her head no, not trusting her voice.

"Is anything missing from your room? Perhaps you surprised a thief who became your attacker?" Kate looked around the room for the first time.

"My suitcase and my backpack have been opened." She said with shock in her voice.

"I only have the one suitcase and backpack," she said walking to the bed. "They contain nothing of value expect maybe my laptop which is still here," she pointed to the computer lying dormant on the small study desk as she walked toward it.

"Please mademoiselle," Jean Micheal said stepping in front of her. "Do not touch anything until we have had a chance to examine it first."

The inspector was forming his next question, when a young policeman entered the room and waited a respectful distance away from the foursome until he caught Jean Michael's attention. Excusing himself he approached the young man who was already standing straight but pulled himself to his full height in a form of solicitude.

The young man quietly relayed something to Jean Michael, then handed him a folded sheet of paper. The inspector thanked him; in reply the policeman saluted and withdrew from the room.

"It would seem that we have solved one mystery only to discover another." He told them as he rejoined the group and opened the piece of paper.

"How so?" Jake asked.

"It would appear your attacker, Mademoiselle Compton, is already known to us. He is a, how do you say, *tueur à gages*?" He uttered the phrase in French, which Platte immediately translated for him.

"Hired killer," Leon said.

"Yes," Jean Michael agreed, "he was a hired killer. Our new mystery is who hired him and equally important to us is to know why?" He regarded Jake as he spoke. "And do you monsieur, have a theory, is that how you say, theory about what has happened here?" Jake just shook his head. It appeared the inspector was trying to come to make up his mind about something.

"I believe it would be best if you were to accompany me, Monsieur Bracken, to the police station so that I may take your formal statement as to how you came to kill this upstanding member of French society. Despite being without your trusty six-shooter." A smile tugged at the corner of his mouth.

"This is necessary, you understand, yes?" Jake nodded indicating not only that he understood, but he would accompany him.

"I believe it would be best if Mademoiselle Compton had somewhere else to spend tonight, where she can be taken care of. Do you agree?" He asked Jake.

"Not to mention a room that has a door," Platte mumbled.

"I could leave one of my men to guard the hallway as well." Jake fished his key card out of his pants pocket and handed it to Platte.

"Take her to my room and stay with her," he ordered.

"*Qui, Mon Capitan*," he said executing a perfect parody of a British Sargent Major's salute. Bracken made a dismissive motion with his good hand towards his forehead acknowledgment, and then he shook his head and pushed Platte's shoulder.

"Now, go," He directed pointing towards the hall.

<<<<< >>>>>

The next morning, Kate woke to find sunlight, filtered by heavy drawn curtains, struggling into the room. At first, she didn't remember where she was, but she finally recalled she was in a hotel a mere three blocks from the Eiffel Tower, in Paris, France. She then remembered that arrogant bastard, Bracken, insisted she stay there because he didn't have time to chase her all over town. But the moment she recalled Jake, the last night before came flooding back.

For some unknown reason, someone had attacked her in the not-so-safe confines of her own hotel room; This was Bracken's room, she remembered. Platte had escorted her here, while Jean Micheal, the police inspector, took Jake to the police department to get his formal statement about the attack, and the man he had killed with his bare hands.

All of her clothes were in her own room, and she had been reluctant to go back and get them herself, nor did she want Leon to leave her alone while he retrieved them. Instead, from somewhere, he produced a blue long-sleeved work shirt for her to sleep in.

As soon as she had changed into it, Platte had a cup of hot tea waiting. She presumed, by both the flavor and now because of the throb in her head, that it had been liberally dosed with brandy. Her last memory of the night before drifting off to sleep, was an image of Leon sitting in a chair, under the lamp in the corner of the room, reading a copy of *Le Monde*.

As she stirred in the bed, she knew the shirt Platte had given her to sleep in was Bracken's, because the sleeves engulfed both her arms entire; if it had been Platte's, the length would have more closely matched that of her own arms.

In addition, the shirt was freshly laundered, but not starched, and likely had been dried in the open air on a clothesline; although a faint hint of Bracken's pipe tobacco still permeated the entire garment.

She recalled seeing Bracken's clothing hanging on a line strung along the back of his tent near in the camp. The image came flooding back into her memory. She had seen them on several occasions during the time he and Platte had been at the dig site. As these thoughts drifted through her mind, she found herself wide-awake just moments after opening her eyes.

Kate reached over to the nightstand and switched on the light. She half-expected to find Platte asleep in the chair where she had last seen him sitting, but as she glanced around the room, she quickly realized that she was alone.   However, something was hanging on the door that sealed off this bedroom from the sitting room on the other side, A handwritten note was taped to the backside of the sitting room door.

WHEN YOU GET UP, KNOCK AND I WILL BUY YOUR BREAKFAST – jake

Without a second thought, she hopped out of the bed, and banged her fist on the door.

She detected movement on the other side of the door, saw it swing open, and Platte's lopsided grin peered out from behind it.

"Ah, the lady has arisen." He said, as he continued to open the door.

"Breakfast?" She asked. He looked at his watch.

"Lunch," he countered. She consulted her own watch and discovered that it was almost 11:30.

"Coffee?" She pleaded.

"Yes!" Platte declared, as he ushered her into the room with a sweeping bow. "You don't talk much when you first get up, do you?" He asked, making his way to a carafe of coffee sitting on a small table in front of the window.

"Not when I'm hung over, I don't," she told him as he poured.

"Cream, sugar, brandy or all three?" He asked.

"Just cream," she said trying and failing to stifle a grin.

"A wise choice," he agreed.

"Why, don't you believe in the hair of the dog?" She wanted to know.

"Oh, I live by it, on a daily basis. However, that isn't why I'd advise against the brandy. I know for an absolute fact that if you put brandy in coffee it curdles the cream," he told her with assurance handing her a large white mug.

"And, I suppose you know this from firsthand experience?" She asked, as she sat down in a chair. Platte just grinned in her direction.

She was halfway through the coffee before it dawned on her that Bracken was missing.

"Where's Jake?" She asked concern that Platte
was going to tell her he was in jail.

"He went down to tell the front desk we need the
rooms a little while longer." He told her. She looked at
him quizzically. "Yep, it means all three of us."
"It seems that while Bracken managed to talk the good
inspector out of tossing us all in the Tower, he did keep
our passports, and told Bracken we couldn't leave until
their investigation was completed."
 "The Tower is in London. In France, they condemn you
to the *guillotine*," she informed him before, as she
returned her attention to her coffee.

"My, you're just full of cheerful thoughts this
morning, aren't you?" Before she could respond Bracken
came into the room carrying Kate's bag and backpack.

"Who's full of cheerful thoughts?" Bracken asked
as he set Kate's bags down on the bed. He eyed Platte.
"I doubt it was you. You're full of lots of things, but not
usually cheerful thoughts."

"Mademoiselle Compton," Leon said, pointing to
Kate, "has been giving me a history lesson." Jake looked
at Kate who just shrugged.

"Can I assume, by the way you're not dressed,"
Jake began to ask, "that you missed breakfast," He
continued, "and let me compliment you, ma'am, on your
taste in sleepwear." He turned again to Platte. "I
suppose you just happened to come across my shirt first
is that it?"

"Actually," Platte began, "no. I just happen to have
a much higher regard of my own stuff than I do yours. I
can assure you I did not agonize over my choice more
than two seconds, at the most." Kate stood when Platte
finished.

"You can have it back, just as soon as I shower."
Bracken waved his bandaged arm in dismissal.

"There's something else," she said, as she walked toward the two men. "I don't think I mentioned it last night but thank you for coming to my rescue." She put her hands on Jake's chest, stood on her tiptoes and kissed him softly.

"Hey, what about me," Platte protested. "I held his coat." She giggled and blew him a kiss as she transited the doorway into the bedroom. "Better keep an eye on that one, she's trying to deal with all this sober," she heard Platte say to Bracken in a stage whisper.

"I would've believed nothing less of the lady," Bracken said to him in reply.

"Brandy?" Platte asked.

"I thought you would never ask," Bracken said, as she pushed the door closed.

CHAPTER SIX

Just Outside of Wills Point, TX

Jake Bracken had inherited the ranch from his maternal grandfather, and his grandfather had inherited it from his grandfather. That's as far back as he had ever bothered to trace his family tree, and that was only because he possessed the deeds from the transfers of ownership.

The genealogy of the Bracken family held little interest for Jake. According to family folklore, his great-great-great grandfather had won the ranch in a poker game. While still yet another rumor claimed that two weeks later the former owner of the ranch shot his distant forefather, for cheating him out of the ranch, attributable to some questions regarding a deck of cards containing more than the regulation number of aces.

But, since the deed had been transferred the week before the shooting, the property had remained with his mother's side of the family. For his troubles, the shooter was rewarded for his attempt to right a perceived wrong on the gallows.

Jake, being familiar with some of the upstanding male characters on both sides of his family, would've taken an even-money bet on the veracity of the claim.

The ranch itself was located between Wills Point and Dallas, Texas. Back when the streets of Dallas were little more than dirt and traveled by horse-drawn wagons, it had encompassed over a thousand acres of land where cattle were bred and raised.

Over the years, and through various economic swings, the size of the spread had been significantly reduced. Initially, in the early 1900s, by the discovery of oil on the ranch, while more recently the discovery by home builders that upwardly mobile Dallas families would tolerate a two-hour commute to and from Metro Dallas for a reasonably-priced share of the American Dream.

By the time the deed had passed to Jake, all that was left of the original ranch were the forty acres where the house and barn sat. Both were built shortly after the Civil War.

He'd been here at home working on the ranch for almost a week. The last three months had been a roller coaster of travel and work. Except for a few days here and there, this was the first chance he'd been able to attend to some of the incessant demands of the place.

The police investigation into the death of the man he'd killed in Dr. Compton's room had taken a grueling three days. Once the authorities were satisfied the death was self-defense, at least of a sort, Inspector Jean Michael, of the 15th District of the Paris Homicide Division, had returned all their passports and allowed them to leave France.

Kate Compton had continued on to the *Institute d'Etudes Politiques de Paris,* while Bracken and Platte caught an American Airlines commercial flight from Charles De Gaulle directly to DFW Airport.

Bracken had run into Platte in Columbia over a month ago, but that had been the only contact he'd had with his friend since Paris. He heard nothing from Kate Compton and didn't expect to. This was the primary reason he was very surprised to see her sitting on his front porch swing, as he drove in from working on the fence line that bounded the ranch.

He waved to Kate, and she returned his greeting as he steered the four-wheeler he was riding, into the barn. As he walked to the front of his house, a distance of several hundred feet, he swatted at the dust on his jeans and shirt with the pair of well-used leather gloves he had been wearing.

"Dr. Compton, it's good to see you again," he said as he mounted the steps and extended his hand. She shook it and looked up at him.

"Sorry about just showing up here unannounced," she began, "but I tried calling a few times, and just got your voice mail," she said to him as she released his hand. "Mr. Platte was kind enough to tell me where you lived when I finally got a hold of him."

"Ah," Bracken responded with understanding and a laugh in his voice, "I see my pal is back in town."

"I needed a break and the only way I could get it was to quit answering my phone," he said addressing the unasked question as to why she could only get his voice mail.

"The only way I can do that is not have the phone with me. I think it's plugged up and charging in my office here at the house." He said, indicating with a nod the interior of the home. "I'm not planning on confirming that theory until sometime Monday." When she did not reply he looked at her and spoke again.

"Anyway," he began, "how about something to drink? It's just a tad warm out here."

"Yes, it is," she said standing up from the porch swing, as Bracken unlocked the front door. He swung it open and gestured for her to precede him into the house.

"All the way to the back," he directed following closely behind her. When she reached the back, as Bracken has called it, she found herself standing in a large airy kitchen with a large wooden table on one side, and a fairly modern kitchen on the other. Jake took two glasses from a cupboard and put them on the table.

"Cold, I have beer, diet soda, water, and iced tea. Pick your poison," he said, moving towards the large double-sided refrigerator.

"Sweet or unsweet tea?" She asked.

"Unsweet"

"Then, I would like some tea, please." Jake nodded, and took one of the glasses to the refrigerator, pressed a LED button on the display panel, and held the glass against the switch in the door that caused the automatic icemaker to dispense ice cubes. He then opened the right-hand door of the refrigerator, removed a clear pitcher of tea, filled the glass, and put it back on the table.

"Sorry, no lemons."

"That's fine," she replied, taking a sip from the glass. "This is good," she said holding up the glass to indicate the iced tea.

"It's sun tea." She gave him a questioning look. "You take tea bags, in this case eight of them, put them in a gallon glass jar filled with water, seal it with the lid, and put it out on the back porch for six to eight hours. The sun heats the water and brews the tea from the bags," he said.

"For reasons, I do not pretend to understand, that produces a cleaner and crisper gallon of tea as opposed to pouring boiling water over the bags, which is how my momma learned me how to make it," he told her as he filled his own glass from the pitcher and took a long drink from it, consuming half the tea in it with one gulp.

He refilled his glass and held the pitcher up in a universal question that usually translated into; do you need more. Kate shook her head no, and Bracken put the pitcher back in the refrigerator. He indicated that she should take a seat at the table, as he pulled a chair out for himself.

"Now that we have paid tribute to the time-honored tradition of cutting the dust of the trail, what brings you to my most humble abode?" Kate took another sip of her tea before responding.

"I have a problem," she began.

"As I recall, the last time we were together you had a problem," he mentioned with a smile. She blushed, and quickly took another sip from her glass.

"I'm sorry, I interrupted, that was rude of me please go on."

"I have a problem," she repeated, looking up at Bracken. He motioned with his hand for her to continue.

"After I presented our findings from the ground penetrating radar to the *Institute d'Etudes Politiques de Paris*," she said in flawless French, "I returned to the dig site in Egypt, where I've been for the last three months as the work has continued."

"As you may recall," she went on, "right before we left, Dr. Mohammed was found dead in his tent." Bracken looked at her, but when he said nothing she continued.

"Since then, two of the diggers have died, and Dr. Rashid, the man who took Dr. Mohammed's place with the Egyptian Department of History and Antiquities, has gone missing."

"I met him, I think. In fact, he was the one who told me Dr. Mohammed had been found dead," Bracken interrupted; "how did the diggers die?"

"No one knows," Kate told him.

"I assume they performed autopsies?"

"Yes, including Dr. Mohammed. The findings were inconclusive. In all three cases, their hearts just stopped. Actually, to be more precise, the report stated their hearts had seized. The government declared them all death by natural causes. This despite the fact all three of them were in good health and had no history of heart problems."

"Is there something at the dig that could causing it?" Bracken inquired. "After all, didn't they discover Lord Carnarvon and Howard Carter died from a parasite they inhaled when they opened Tutankhamen's tomb?"

"Actually, it was septicemia, but yes, they did, and the government took all the proper precautions. They suspended the dig and ran a complete series of toxicology tests on the air, soil, and water, which all came back negative."

"I agree that it's unusual, but people die all the time," Bracken said with a shrug. "Overwork, incessant heat and poor health otherwise. Most of the common laborers appeared to be pretty persistently malnourished." Kate gave him a withering look before commenting.

"We do our best to feed the workers well. It's hard and physically demanding work. We make sure not only are the workers fed but, we feed them a high-calorie diet because the work is so physical."

"I wasn't accusing you of anything," Bracken said, "just making an observation." After he spoke, he took another drink from his glass, and Kate nodded her understanding.

"When did Dr. Rashid disappear?"

"Three weeks ago," she replied. "He said he was going to visit another part of the site to check on something. We thought nothing of it at the time, even though his destination wasn't where we were working. At dinner that night, someone noticed he never showed up."

"And he was reported missing?" Bracken asked.

"Yes, and once more the dig was shut down while there was a search an investigation," she answered. "They found no trace of him."

"Could he have gotten lost and wandered away from the camp, into the open desert?" Bracken asked, before taking another drink from his glass.

"Not likely," Kate said rather dismissively. "He was a seasoned researcher and intimately familiar with the dangers of the desert. The National Police searched within a five-mile radius from the base camp and even put drones up and went fifty miles out beyond that." Bracken again motioned for her to continue.

"Nothing," she simply replied.

"Nothing as in, they didn't find him, or nothing as in, they found no indication as to where he had gone?" Bracken inquired.

"Both," she said, "or rather neither. They didn't find any trace of him at all. Nothing. Nada. He just vanished into thin air."

The room was silent as they both pondered the melting ice in their glasses and Bracken considered how to broach a sensitive subject.

"Has anyone," he began apprehensively, slowly rotating his glass in his hands, "connected the attack on you in Paris with what's happening in Egypt?" Taken aback, Kate raised her head in astonishment, and met

Bracken's gaze with bewilderment as she recalled the attack on her in the darkened hotel room in Paris.

"No," she said, after taking a moment to steady her emotions, "you don't really think one has anything to do with the other, do you?"

"I think it would be incomprehensible not to connect them," Bracken replied evenly. "During the last conversation I had with Jean Michael a month ago, he told me the police had yet to find a motive for your attack." He paused tilting his head to one side.

"There's still something that puzzles me about that whole incident."

"What's that?" Kate asked after another sip of her tea.

"How did your attacker, or whoever hired him, know where you were staying?" He asked. Kate reflected on that for a moment before answering,

"Didn't you make reservations? They had rooms ready for us when we got there," she reasoned.

"Well, yes and no," he said tilting his hand, palm down, back and forth. "I'd emailed Solaris Travel the night before and told them I need three rooms. The Hilton is where Solaris usually puts people up when they're in Paris, but I just said I needed three rooms. I didn't give them our names just that I needed three rooms. Names weren't attached to the reservation until we checked in."

Kate mulled this over, while Bracken watched her. When she couldn't come up a reasonable explanation she looked back at Jake.

"The answer," he supplied, "is someone followed us from Orly." He let that sink in for a moment, before continuing. "Which means," he said drawing it out, "someone had to know that we were going to Paris, that we were going by private aircraft, and that we were going to Orly."

"But who?" She asked.

"Good question," Bracken replied. "As far as I know only three people knew how and where we were traveling, Platte, you, and me."

"And Lester," Kate whispered. When she realized she had used his first name she corrected herself. "I mean Dr. Walker. He knew because he was the one who told me that you were leaving as soon as the police released the camp and you were going to Paris."

"How did he know?" Bracken asked.

"I just assumed Mr. Platte told him," she replied. Bracken paused and considered what she had just said.

"OK," he said, still not sure he was ready to accept that explanation. "That still doesn't explain how they knew how we were getting there or that that we were going to Orly." Kate thought it over.

"Didn't you file a route? Oh, what do you call it…a flight plan?" She asked, finally recalling the term.

"Yes, I filed a flight plan through Solaris the night before too," Jake said, deliberating slowly as he answered.

"That's public record isn't it?"

"It's, only…" he stopped, letting what he'd been thinking catch up with him, "you have to know to look for it and you have to know what you're looking for. It won't pop up doing a Google search."

They both sat motionless as Jake turned over in his mind what they had just discussed and Kate, watching Jake.

"So," he murmured as much to himself as to Kate, "Dr. Mohammed is found dead in his tent at the base camp. Someone who knew when, where, and how we were getting there, attacks you in Paris. Two additional people are dead, and now one person is missing."

"Two," Kate said.

"What?" Bracken asked, dumbfounded by her response.

"There are two people missing. That's what I came here to tell you, Dr. Walker's missing now too."

CHAPTER SEVEN

Just Outside of Wills Point, TX

"So, that's your problem?" Bracken asked. Kate slowly nodded her head. Bracken didn't reply for a moment.

"Well," he finally declared, "that's a problem alright, but it doesn't explain why you're here with your problem," he emphasized you and your. Kate dropped her gaze to the table; then she looked up with a new resolve in her eyes.

"With Dr. Walker missing, I am…well…," she told him, "in charge of the dig. I flew into Dallas two days ago. I went to the University and arranged a meeting with the President this morning I asked him to ask your boss, Mr. Coleman, to send you and Mr. Platte to help me."

"And just how do you know he's going to comply with your request and send us back to the desert?" Bracken asked with a smile.

"Well, first, the President's daughter is married to Mr. Coleman's son," Kate responded as the smile vanished from Bracken's face.

"And your second reason?" He asked.

"They also share a Skybox at the Cowboy Stadium?" She stated as an is-that-enough question to Jake. Bracken thought this over for a moment, before commenting.

"Well, blood ties are one thing," he paused, his smile returning to his face, "sharing Cowboys games is what is known, in this part of the world anyway, as a lifetime commitment," Bracken got up from the table and walked out of the kitchen. When he returned, he was scrolling through the screen of his phone.

"Guess who I have three phone calls and voice messages from?" Bracken asked, as he reentered the kitchen. Kate smiled at him self-consciously. He continued scrolling through the phone. He paused, stabbed at the screen, and moved the receiver to his ear.

"I hear you're in Dallas," he said without greeting. He paused to listen before he responded. "Yea, I know; she's sitting here in my kitchen now." At that point it finally dawned on Kate he was talking to Leon Platte.

"Yea, I know that too; I got calls and messages from him. Unlike the rest of this modern world, my phone is not a permanent appendage to my body, and I don't all ways keep it with me." He halted and listened before taking up his side of the conversation once more.

"Well, since she and I are both together already, it would be best if you come here too. No, I'm not going to feed you. You can stop at Drovers and get something. I do have beer." He sat back down at the table while he listened, then he chuckled into the phone.

"Yes, it's cold beer," After another short pause he answered again. "Sausage. I don't know; I'll ask her."

"Beef, pork, or chicken?" He asked. She answered almost immediately.

"Pork. Ribs," she said decisively.

"Pork ribs she said." Following another short pause, "I don't know that either; get some of each, I guess. Yea, I'm sure it's cold; don't worry," he chuckled. "Yea, you too." Bracken stabbed at the phone to disconnect the call. He shot Kate a quizzical look.

"Their chicken's always too dry," she said in response to his unasked question. Bracken just shook his head; then scrolled back through the phone and poked the screen again.

She could hear the other end of the line ringing when Bracken put the phone back to his ear. She assumed the number he was calling had been answered when he immediately asked to speak to Mr. Coleman.

There was a delay of almost a minute before Bracken said "hello, sir" and then listened respectfully.

When he did finally join into the conversation, he told Mr. Coleman that he was indeed sorry to have missed his calls, but he had been out on 'the ranch' and didn't get much of a signal out there, giving Kate a conspiratorial wink. What followed was a rather one-sided conversation, with Bracken doing most of the listening.

When he finally got a word in edgewise, he advised Mr. Coleman that Kate had already been in contact with him; and yes, he understood he was being dispatched back to Egypt, as soon as he could make the necessary arrangements.

"I'm taking Platte with me," Bracken said. He listened again before commenting. "Because I need him, that's why. He's familiar with the equipment, and he knows where they were working, I trust him to watch my back, and I need a co-pilot." He listened again, grinned at Kate and then terminated the call.

"All set," he told her placing his phone on the table and looking at his watch.

"Platte's gonna be here in an hour or so. I've been working outside all day, and I smell like it. I need to put some stuff up in the barn and I'd really like to take a shower before he gets here." He motioned for her to follow him back the way they had come when they entered the house.

Kate rose from the table and followed Jake to what she assumed was his office.

It was a spacious and sizeable room, at least 15 feet wide by 20 feet long. It had three large windows that afforded an encompassing view of the open part of the ranch. As she faced the windows, on her right, stood a large desk with assorted papers scattered on the surface. Dominating most of the desktop space was an oversized computer monitor, keyboard, and a mouse on a mouse pad featuring a picture of Tigger, from *Winnie The Pooh*, which made her smile.

The left side of the room accommodated a couch and two chairs arranged around a coffee table and featured a huge television screen. The furniture appeared comfortable and seemed to fit both the room and Jake's personality.

What captured most of Kate's attention were the bookshelves. The long wall directly across from the windows and the shorter wall behind the desk were covered in floor-to-ceiling bookshelves.

Bracken approached the coffee table and motioned with his hand inviting her to take a seat. He picked up a remote, pointed it at the television and pressed the power button.

"I think you'll be more comfortable here," he said. "Please make yourself at home, while I get done outside and grab a shower. You know where the refrigerator is; help yourself to more tea or anything else that strikes your fancy. I should be back in about the time Platte gets here." He handed her the remote and then walked out of the room.

Kate sat down, but only long enough to turn the television off. As soon as the screen went black, she walked to the bookshelves on the long wall of the room.

The shelves housed a mixed collection of books, memorabilia, knick-knacks, and plaques sharing the space around the room. By far, the large number of books overwhelmed the space.

As expected, she found a variety of books about aviation and flying. Also, as expected, she found volumes related to the petrochemical industry, but not as many as she had thought she might. What did surprise her was the vast scope of topics the rest of the books encompassed.

There were books covering nearly every period of history over the last four thousand years; although there was a wider selection about World War Two in both Europe and the Pacific than anything else, she found.

She found novels, classic works, and recent best sellers; but what seemed to appropriate the greatest amount of shelf space were science fiction books.

Fully a third were written between 1945 and 1960, which were older and more dilapidated and appeared to have been unearthed at garage sales or recused from dumpsters.

Handfuls were penned at the end of the 1800s and early 1900s; books by Jules Vern, Edgar Rice Boroughs, and H. G. Wells. There was even a collection of science fiction short stories written by Sir Arthur Conan Doyle, the creator of Sherlock Holmes.

Kate moved to the shorter wall and found more, recent books of science fiction, computer books, and a sizable collection of atlases. For almost an hour she moved back and forth from wall to wall marveling at Bracken's collection.

"I bet you didn't even think he could read something that didn't have a foldout in the middle?" Startled, Kate spun around to find Leon Platte standing in the doorway holding two plastic carryout bags by the handles.

"You scared me," she said regaining her composure. "I didn't hear you come in."

"I can be very stealthy when I'm hungry and sober," he told her and disappeared down the hall. Without a second thought she followed him back to the kitchen.

By the time she caught up with him, he had put the bags on the kitchen table and was opening two brown beer bottles. He handed one of them to Kate and then took a long pull from the neck of the bottle he kept for himself.

Platte was wearing a pair of jeans shorts displaying a wide pallet of paint colors, a faded blue t-shirt promoting the Fort Worth Stockyards, and a battered pair of sneakers without socks.

He suppressed a belch and moved to the cupboard removing plates and handing them to Kate. He then went back to the kitchen counter and opened a drawer, fishing out a handful of silverware, then walked past Kate to the table, just as Bracken appeared in the doorway.

Bracken's hair was still damp from the shower, although it did show signs of having had a comb run through it. He had traded the jeans and work shirt for a pair of beige Dockers and a white knit polo shirt.

"I see you found the beer," Bracken said to Platte as he entered the kitchen and headed towards the refrigerator. Leon just smiled, and saluted Jake with his now half-empty bottle.

"That's not a good idea," Platte advised, retrieving the plates from Kate who was still holding them. He plunked the plates down on the table and with a great deal of racket dropped the silverware, onto the plates; all the while still clutching his beer bottle.

"What's not a good idea?" Bracken asked.

"Eatin' bar-b-que in a white shirt," he told Jake as Bracken pulled his own bottle of beer from the refrigerator.

"I know how to use a napkin," Bracken responded, motioning Kate to the table.

"You're my witness," Platte said, looking at Kate. "I warned him."

"I vote we eat first, talk later," Platte announced, taking Styrofoam containers from the bags on the table while Bracken organized the plates and silverware.

The feast, at least that's how Kate thought of it, consisted of potato salad, corn on the cob, cowboy beans, sliced sausage links, and generous portions of pork spareribs. Each of them served their own plate, and as Platte suggested, ate without much conversation. The only disruption occurred when Platte fetched three more bottles of beer to the table.

"I'm amazed," Platte said, pushing his plate a few inches back from the edge of the table.

"About?" Bracken asked, pulling a paper towel that he had used as a bib from the collar of his shirt.

"Your shirt. It's still white."

"We all have our methods. I admire yours too, by the way." Platte shot him a quizzical look before Bracken continued. "I admire how you disguise the bar-b-que stains in the midst of all the other crap you've spilled on that shirt." Platte feigned indignation and proceeded to flip Bracken off.

Platte then rose from the table and gathered up plates, silverware, and Styrofoam containers, and took them to the other side of the kitchen. Bracken stood up and followed him.

In a matter of minutes Platte was rinsing plates and silverware, albeit quite noisily, and placing them in the dishwasher. Meanwhile, Bracken arranged the leftovers in the refrigerator and started a pot of coffee.

Platte caught Kate's attention and held up a fresh unopened bottle of beer. She shook her head no. He just shrugged and walked out of the kitchen with his bottle.

When he returned, just a few minutes later, Bracken was walking to the table with two steaming cups of fresh coffee. He placed one in front of Kate and put the other where he had been sitting.

"Cream and sugar?" Bracken asked.

"Cream, thank you." She said as Platte took his seat at the table. She couldn't help noticing his new bottle of beer was already half empty. Bracken returned and placed a carton of half and half and a spoon down in front of her.

"Paying the rent on the beer," Platte said, explaining his brief absences. After he was seated Bracken quickly recounted his earlier conversation with Kate.

"So, we're going back to the land of Ra?" Leon asked.

"That is what I've been, very bluntly, ordered to do," Bracken said after taking a cautious sip of his coffee still- too-hot coffee. "But what I want to know is; why? Or more precisely, why us?" He asked scrutinizing Kate. After a long pause, she explained as best she could.

"Well, when we were in Paris, waiting for you to come down for dinner, Mr. Platte..." she began.

"Leon, please, my dear," he said patting her hand.

"Leon," she began again, "told me how you seemed to be able to discover what was really going in the places Solaris sends you. Leon supposed that's why your boss sends you to some of those places." Bracken instantly shifted a hard look in Platte's direction.

"Oops," Leon uttered, taking a quick pull from the neck of his beer bottle. Kate paused uncomfortably, shifting her attention back and forth between the two men. At length, Bracken turned his attention back to Kate, and motioned for her to continue.

"I'm very afraid, with Dr. Walker's disappearance, they're going to shut down our dig."

"Who's 'they'?" Leon asked.

"The Egyptian Department of History and Antiquities," she said in reply before adding "and the University as well. The Egyptians are very sensitive about bad publicity at archeological sites. Between the fees we pay to be there and the money from tourism, these digs are big cash cows for their government."

"I'll bet the University is equally touchy about misplacing a skinny professor in the desert too," Leon said to no one in particular.

"What can we do," Bracken asked, "that the authorities aren't already doing or haven't already done?"

"The authorities aren't interested in finding out what really happened. They're convinced the diggers died from natural causes and that Dr. Rashid got lost in the desert," she replied.

"They have no desire to find out what really happened, they just want all of it to go away. And now, with Dr. Walker's disappearance, the best way to accomplish that is to force us all to go away. I want to prevent that at all cost."

"And I need to know if Dr. Walker is still alive."

Bracken leaned back in his chair and stared at the ceiling. When he looked back down, he informed Platte of his belief that the attack on Kate in Paris and the troubles in Egypt were somehow all connected. Platte pondered this information before responding.

"Was it Sherlock Holmes, Dick Tracy, or Jay Leno who said 'there are no such thing as coincidences'?"

"Exactly," Bracken acknowledged.

"So," Platte began, "what provoked all of this?" Bracken caught Platte's attention and motioned with his hand for him to continue with that train of thought.

"What connected Dr. Mohammad, you," he said, pointing to Kate, "two common laborers, Dr. Rashid, and Dr. Walker?"

"The dig?" Kate offered.

"OK," replied Platte, "but what specifically about the dig?" There was a long pause while everyone contemplated his question. Bracken folded his hands onto the table and proposed a solution.

"The soundings," Bracken said, in a low even voice. Kate raised her eyebrows quizzically.

"The soundings," Platte repeated. "The scans from the ground penetrating radar I was there to train your team how to use. We spent two days working a good distance away from your dig site so I could show your folks how to use the equipment, calibrate it to the depths your guys were most interested in plumbing." Platte said thinking back.

"The next day we moved inside your dig area to places you'd already been working, just to make sure the scans revealed what you knew was already there. It was sorta a final check on the equipment and to makes sure everyone knew how to operate it."

"What happened to the data after it was collected?" Bracken asked Platte. Platte pointed across the table, deferring to Kate.

"I took all the data from each shot and burned copies on DVDs," Kate said. "One copy goes to the University of Texas; two copies went to Dr. Mohammed. I kept two copies-one for documentation and one for Dr. Walker," she told them. "It's standard procedure."

"Did you look at them?" Bracken asked Kate.

"Just enough to verify that the data had been transferred to the DVDs," she said with a shrug. "I don't analyze them; Dr. Walker and Dr. Mohammed do that. Well," she paused, "did that."

"How?" Bracken continued.

"I'm not exactly sure but," she said, "I would give one DVD to each of them. Dr. Walker would review the scans to determine where we should concentrate our efforts. Then he would submit his request to Dr. Mohammad, who would compare our request to a grid map."

"What kinda grid map?" Bracken asked.

"Aerial, or in some cases, satellite photos are taken of both the upper and lower Nile Valley that are considered of archeological significance," she explained.

"Then, The Egyptian Department of History and Antiquities overlays the photos with a Cartesian Coordinated System of x and y axis to form grids. Finally, each grid is assigned a three-or-four-digit alphanumeric code. I think computers do it all now."

"Then what happens?" Bracken asked.

"If there were no issues with the locations Dr. Walker had requested to work in, then Dr. Mohammad would give us permission. Normally by means of an email that he cc'd to the Egyptian Department of History and Antiquities.

"Did he ever turn down a request?" Platte asked, reentering the conversation.

"Rarely, if ever that I'm aware of," Kate replied. " I can't recall a single time in the last three years when he's turned Dr. Walker down. It's a fairly routine exchange; Dr. Walker asks, and Dr. Mohammad approves."

"I think it's more a process to keep track of where people are working." Kate looked back and forth between Bracken and Platte, both of whom seemed to be lost in their own thoughts for the moment. Finally, Bracken broke his reverie by suddenly jumping up from the table and walking out of the kitchen.

Kate shot Platte a questioning look. He just shrugged in an I-have-no-idea answer. When Bracken returned just a few moments later he was carrying one of the many atlases she had seen earlier in his office. He flipped the book open, to a place marked with a pencil and slid it across the table in front of Leon.

"Base camp was here," Bracken said, marking a spot on the exposed map page with the pencil. As he did so Kate got up and moved around the table so she could see what Jake and Leon were looking at.

"Your team," he said, directing his attention to Kate, "was working here?" He asked, while making another mark on the map. She leaned over the table and scrutinized the placement of the pencil mark.

"More or less about there, yes," she said to him. Bracken handed the pencil to Leon.

"Show me where you did the calibration test soundings?" Platte took the proffered pencil and leaned over the book. Using the end of the pencil as a pointer, he started at the base camp, moved it to the dig site, and then shifted it left in an almost a straight line, a short distance from the dig site.

"Here," Platte said, drawing an X where he stopped the pencil, "about a 200 to 400 meters from the dig."

"And you took production shots at the dig site on the third day after you finished calibration and training the team on how to use the system?" Bracken asked, pointing to the dig site with his finger. Platte nodded his agreement.

"We tested there," Platte said, pointing with the pencil, "for two days. Then we moved to the dig site. During the morning of the third day, I made shots and showed them how to use the equipment. By that afternoon, they were making the shots and I supervised."

"Then on the morning of the fourth day, I checked in with them, just to make sure they didn't have any more questions, I watched them make a shot, then I left, which is when I met up with you and told you we could leave." Bracken mulled this over before continuing.

"How did you record the reading from the shots?" Bracken asked.

"On a laptop, like we always do," Platte told him. "She," he said, pointing to Kate, "gave it to me before I started the calibration shots."

"What did you do with the laptop at the end of the day?"

"The first night," Platte replied, "I disconnected it and put it in the storage box on the mortar. The second night, I took it back to my tent to review the calibration.

"And the third night? "

"I gave it to Kate." He said nodding in her direction. "I told her we were going to start working the dig site that morning and she asked me to bring it back to her that night when we were done." Bracken turned his attention towards Kate.

"Leon told me they were going to start doing production shots," she said without being asked. "Dr. Mohammad and Dr. Walker were both quite anxious to see the scans, because the equipment Solaris loaned us was state-of-the-art and so much more accurate than what we had been using. Everyone was eager to see how good the resolution was." Bracken started to say something, but Platte interrupted.

"Actually, it wasn't 'that night' exactly. We had worked through lunch, and a couple of the girls on the team were starting to fade; no lunch and the heat, I guess. We knocked off about two."

"That's right," Kate confirmed. "Leon brought the laptop to me shortly after lunch. I immediately transferred copies of the data and the scans on to DVD disk. I personally took one to Dr. Mohammad and one to Dr. Walker." Bracken paused to digest what Kate and Platte had just said. Then he turned back to Kate.

"Do you know if they looked at the files?"

"I know Dr. Mohammad did. As soon as I gave him the disc, he immediately loaded it into his laptop and started looking through them."

"And Dr. Walker?"

"He wasn't in his tent when I took the disc to him, so I just left it on his laptop. I'm assuming he looked at them later."

Bracken got up, collected his coffee cup and Kate's, and walked to the counter. He filled both cups and started back to the table. As he approached the refrigerator Platte got his attention.

"Since you're up," he said, waving his now-empty beer bottle. Bracken brought the coffee to the table, put both cups down and retreated to the refrigerator. He fished out another bottle of beer, opened it, and handed it to Platte before retaking his seat at the table. He looked directly back at Kate.

"I need you to think this through carefully and be certain about your answer," he said to her. Concern crossed her face before she nodded.

"Whose idea was it to send you to Paris?" She put down her coffee cup and closed her eyes thinking back. When she opened them she responded.

"Dr. Walker's."

"Why did he want you to go to Paris?" Bracken asked her in an even voice. She thought for a moment recalling the conversation she had with her boss.

"Dr. Walker said there were anomalies in the scans he'd looked at, and he wanted them enhanced so he could get a better idea of what he was seeing. *Politiques* was the closest place to us to have that done."

"Was that a standard practice?" Bracken wanted to know. Kate shook her head.

"Standard, no, but we'd sent them things to analyze for us before. But," she hesitated, "this was the first time anyone had physically delivered the scans to them. Usually, we just transferred them digitally through the University's server."

"And how did you take the scans with you to Paris?"

"They were on the laptop. I burned a copy onto a blank DVD before I left the hotel." She told him.

"Where are the files now?" Bracken asked her.

"On my laptop. It's in the car." She said indicating the front of the house.

"Did they complete the enhancements you needed?" She nodded. "Do you have those with you?" Again, she nodded.

"I need a copy of all of them. The originals and the enhanced scans." Bracken told her.

"Sure." She said with a shrug. "But they won't do you any good."

"Why not?" Bracken asked.

“They don’t have the grid markings on them. Dr. Rashid hadn’t gotten around to overlaying them before he vanished.”

“Oh, don’t worry about that,” he said, leaning back in his chair. “I can get them read and gridded.”

CHAPTER EIGHT

Solaris Headquarters – Dallas, TX

Oil companies no longer rely on rough, callous, and self-sufficient Texas oilmen commonly known as wildcatters, to find new oil reserves. Finding oil in the 21st Century is, predominantly an uneasy marriage between money and geology. Vast and ever-increasing sums of money are consumed in the search for untapped oil reserves.

In the last fifteen years, most of the oil extracted from the ground in the United States, has been accomplished using two new methods of obtaining the fabled black gold. The first is known as the 'horizontal' drilling method.

A vertical, or traditional straight-down oil shaft, is drilled into the rock strata. Then numerous horizontal shafts, or slants, as they are called, are drilled to facilitate the release of additional oil and natural gas over a widespread area sometimes extending countless miles from the original shaft.

A traditional oil well can now easily embody dozens of slants drilled from the same well, each producing oil or natural gas.

The second method in extensive use is known as hydraulic fracturing or fracking. Ninety percent of oil and natural gas wrestled out of the ground in the United States today is done using the fracking method in conjunction with horizontal drilling.

A traditional oil well is drilled thousands of feet into the ground until it enters a specific rock stratum known as shale.

Shale is a fine-grained sedimentary rock that is created when silt and clay mineral particles mix.

Technically, shale is a sedimentary rock known as mudstones. Shale is distinguished from other mudstones because it is fissile and laminated. Laminated means that the rock is comprised of many thin layers; fissile means that the rock readily splits into thin pieces along the laminations.

Shale rock is normally located in huge areas known as basins. The shale formations themselves, can cover thousands of square miles, and are contained within the basins. Two of the most commonly known shale formations are the Barnett Shale and the Marcellus Shale.

The Barnett Shale covers an area from Ft. Worth north to the Texas/Oklahoma state line and from the outskirts of the eastern edge of Dallas west to San Angelo.

The Marcellus Shale is the largest known shale basin in the United States. It runs from the western part of the state of New York all the way south through the western half of Pennsylvania and encompasses most if not all of the state of West Virginia.

Millions, if not billions, of barrels of oil, are trapped in the shale rock; in most cases in the same areas it was located and extracted decades ago using traditional methods, it wasn't until the late 1990s that oil companies developed a method of extracting oil trapped in the shale formations surrounding the older legacy drilling sites.

After a traditional vertical well is drilled down to the shale strata then horizontal shafts are drilled in all directions into the shale. Then, small explosive charges are pushed down and along the drill shafts and exploded. The result is fracturing, or fracking, of small fissures in the shale around the horizontal shafts, releasing crude oil and natural gas.

At that point, a mixture of mainly water and sand, commonly called mud or slip, is pumped into the well to keep the cracks open and to facilitate the flow of oil and natural gas up the main shaft.

The price of oil and natural gas in the world markets fluctuates on a daily basis. When the price of oil is down oil companies can still drill fracked wells. However, fracked wells can be brought into production, or removed based on the price of oil as opposed to the cost of production.

The process that used to take months is now measured in days. Unlike traditional vertical oil wells, that take months to drill, and even longer to bring online, fracking wells can and are drilled quickly and brought into production in a very short time frame.

As oil companies watch the price of oil drop, they can leave the crude and natural gas in the well, a process known as in-ground storage, until the price rises.

While drilling techniques and oil extraction methods have greatly improved in the last two decades, oil companies would be lost without the third variable of the oil drilling equation; computer technology.

Third, only to the cost of drilling rights, the drilling equipment, oil companies willingly spend hundreds of millions of dollars annually on computer hardware and software. Oil exploration companies in particular are some of the most prominent investors in artificial intelligence, or AI.

In addition to the mundane functions of email, word processing, and personnel, computers are harnessed for everything from where to position their rigs, how deep to drill, and even how fast to spin the drill bit as it drills.

Satellite imagery, the results of ground-penetrating radar, geology, and weather conditions are all analyzed in concert by sophisticated computer systems that give oil companies critical information about where they can find and drill for oil. Solaris Oil was no exception and, as a result of prudent investments, owned one of the most extensive and complex systems in the world.

Consequently, just as any other tool or piece of equipment, a computer, regardless of how intelligent, is only as good as the people who use, program, and run them. At Solaris, the task of managing their massive computer investment falls under the watchful eyes of one woman: Dr. Karen Hauser.

Karen Hauser had worked for Solaris for over 30 years. Always on the hunt for talent Solaris recognized her abilities when she was a secretary in the company's main office. As with all the other aspects of their business, Solaris understood the value of investing in people, as well as equipment. The company not only paid for her to college tuition, but they also paid her while she attended school. Over 15 years, Karen earned both a PhD in computer sciences and one in geology.

Dr. Hauser looked up from a detailed geological report she'd been reading for the last few hours when she heard a rap on her opened office door. She looked up over her glasses and her face broke out into a beaming smile, as she recognized Jake Bracken leaning against the doorframe.

"Hiya Doc," he said reflecting her smile as he entered her office. Karen quickly got up from her desk, and met Jake halfway, enveloping him in a hug.

"As I live and breath, if it isn't the last of the great Texas sheepherders," she exclaimed, evoking their private joke. Sheepherders in Texas Cattle County are about as welcomed as pork chops at a kosher wedding. She broke their embrace and motioned towards a round table on the other side of her office.

Jake Bracken was one of Karen Hauser's favorite people. They'd met at a party hosted by mutual friends years before. They laughed when they discovered they worked for the same company after they were introduced to each other. Karen was immediately impressed with Jake, not by the things he knew but by his ready admission to things he didn't know.

The party ended with Karen giving Jake a very genuine invitation to come and see her at Solaris' headquarters. Taking her at her word, Jake showed up the next afternoon. It was the first of many times the two spend time together, both in and out of work. A close friendship quickly formed between them and continued to deepen over the years.

One of the many things Karen appreciated about him was the fact that Jake afforded her an enormous amount of respect for her intelligence and the major role she played at Solaris. On more than one occasion, Jake had stopped by her office and asked her a specific question about how some aspect of the well-to-market process of drilling for oil worked. Not only did he ask intelligent questions, but also, he listened intently when she answered him.

Sometime gossip would filter back to her about a major shakeup that had ensued at one of Solaris' operations after Jake had been there. Often as not, the changes were rumored to be tied to something Jake had asked her about in the preceding weeks.

"Have you ever worried," Jake asked motioning outside the glass walls of her office to the racks of servers, "that all the electricity you pull in here has fooled you into thinking you have naturally curly hair?"

"It had occasionally crossed my mind, until I happened to see my first-grade class picture where I exhibited beautifully curly red hair and no front teeth to speak of," she said with an exaggerated flip of her hair. This triggered a laugh from Jake.

"Much as I would like to believe you just happened by in a desire to gaze upon my curls," she looked at Jake and winked, "I know better. What can I do for my favorite sheepherder today?"

In reply he reached into the backpack he had removed from his left shoulder when he entered the room and fished out the DVD, secured in a transparent jewel case, Kate Compton had given him the day before, and slid it across the table.

"I need a wide sector detail of the data mapped on here with and L and L grid map overlaid. I also need a side view of each topical view as well." Karen picked up the disc and turned it over in her hands.

"And where is here?" she asked.

"Valley of the Kings, Egypt," he answered. "More specifically, the archeological dig UT is doing that Solaris is funding. Those," he nodded to the disc, "are the seismic reading taken from the first few days of shots Platte did when we were in Egypt three months ago."

"And what are we looking for specifically?"

"I'm not sure," Jake said with a shrug. "That's why I would like it all mapped and overlaid."   Without commenting Karen picked up the phone on her desk, dialed four numbers, paused, and asked the person on the other end of the line to please come to her office.

A few moments later, a very professionally dressed young woman in her mid-twenties appeared in the office. Jake rose from his chair.

"Mandy Burgess meet Jake Bracken," Jake extended his hand and Mandy shook it. "Mandy joined us from the University of Oklahoma a few months ago," Karen said nodding towards the young lady. "Mandy, this is Jake Bracken, the last of the great Texas sheepherders." Mandy smiled as Jake released her hand. Karen extended the disc to Mandy.

"Please have the data on here analyzed and then plotted in a wide sector map with a latitude and longitude map overlaid on the topical results, and with a side view of each as well?" She looked at Bracken. "What increments?" She asked him. Jake thought for a moment before answering.

"Fives," he decided.

"In five-meter increments, please," Karen, said looking at her watch. "And can you have it done in say, ninety minutes? That's when we should be back from lunch, which Mr. Bracken kindly invited me to."

"No problem, Dr. Hauser," she said as she turned to leave.

"Ms. Burgess," Jake called after her. She paused and turned to face him. "There are a couple of days of test and calibration shots at the start of the data on the disc. Would you map and overlay those as well?" Jake asked. Karen nodded her approval to Mandy. Jake watched as the younger woman left the room.

"Remember when the girls were awestruck to meet the famous swashbuckling Solaris flyboy?" Karen asked, rising from her seat. Jake sighed in mocked resignation.

"Alas, no one is impressed with an old Texas sheepherder anymore," he replied, smiling at her. She patted him on the arm in consolation as she joined him.

"It was very nice of you to ask me to lunch," she said, looping her arm into Jake's. Jake laughed, as he escorted Karen through the door to her office.

When they returned, close to two hours later, Karen was not surprised to find a three and a half foot long black plastic tube with screw-on caps at each end, and the disc Jake had given Karen earlier, sitting on her desk.   She handed both items to him.

"Aren't you going to check?" she asked as he put the disc in his backpack and tucked the tube under his arm.

"Nope," Jake said smiling. "Ms. Burgess wouldn't be working for you if I had to check." Karen smiled back at his vote of confidence. She kissed Jake on the cheek.

"You be careful," she told him, "Egypt is a long way off and as you well know, not all sheepherders are as trustworthy as you are, although I still have my doubt about you."

"It's always good to have doubts," Jake said to her as he walked to the door, "it's what keeps you human."

"Have you looked at these yet?" Platte asked Jake several hours later as he and Kate Compton studied the maps Dr. Hauser had provided to Bracken. The maps were spread out on the table in Bracken's kitchen, the ends held down by bottles of beer. Kate had earlier questioned Platte as to the wisdom of using beer bottles to hold down the maps.

"Won't the condensation ruin the map when the bottles sweat?" She asked as Platte placed them on the paper. He looked up at her from his task before replying.

"They're not cold, which means they ain't gonna condensate on the maps," he told her looking back down. "It also renders them pretty unfit for any other use, especially drinking." It was then Kate realized Platte's point of view was concerned with the beer, not the maps.

"Yes," Bracken said, "as soon as I got back from Puzzle Palace. These," he said, pointing to a stack of maps on the left side of the table, "are from here." He pointed to the Atlas they had been using the day before. "Where you ran the test and calibration shots."

"And these?" Platte wanted to know as he pointed to another stack of maps.

"Are from the shots you did with Kate's team after you had it calibrated," Bracken replied.

"What's this?" Kate pointed to the maps from the test shots.

"Oh, you spotted that, did you?" Bracken smiled at her.

"They take up almost the bottom half of the page," she replied, "so they're kinda hard to miss." She pointed to the charts Platte was leaning over.

"It's a tunnel," Platte said, not looking up, "and a huge one at that."

"Then what are these above it?" she pointed to several areas on the side view maps that were positioned above the tunnel and had the same appearance on the map as the tunnel itself, indicating open areas.

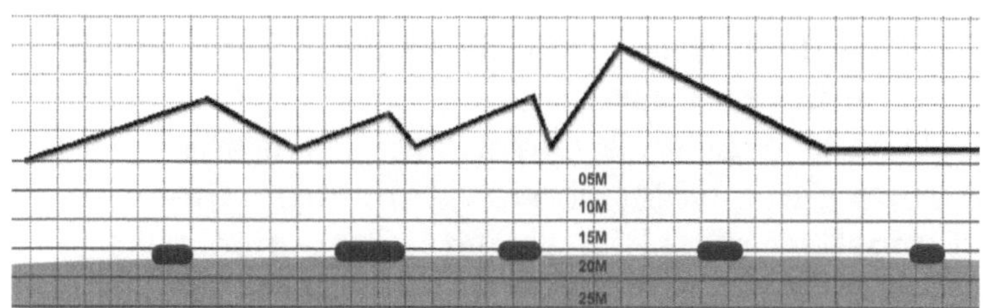

"Good question." Bracken acknowledged. "It looks like they're openings, rooms or chambers, cut above the tunnel, and," he said pointing to the side view chart, "they were done at a later date."

"How can you tell?" She wanted to know.

"Because," Jake said, pointing to the map again, "the newer sections show up darker than the old ones." Platte stood up.

"And I suppose you researched the tunnels?" Platte asked looking at Bracken. Before he could answer Kate spoke up.

"Water!" she exclaimed.

"That was my guess too." Bracken nodded.

"Water?" Bracken used his hand to invite Kate to answer Platte's question.

"Over the course of history, from time to time during the growing seasons, there would be a drought. The regional farms depended on rains in the south of the Nile valley to bring the water they need upstream for irrigation." She looked down at the map again. "We heard myths and legends that several times tunnels had been dug to bring water from the Nile onto the farms to provide for irrigation."

"But everyone assumed the tunnels would have been filled in over the years or even more than likely, the existence of the tunnels was nothing more than folklore," she almost whispered, as she continued to look at the chart.

"Why dig tunnels?" Platte asked. "Why not a ditch? It had to be easier"

"The Nile valley is surrounded by dessert. If they had tried to move water above ground from the Nile inland, most, if not all of it, would have evaporated by the time it reached the farmland."

"So, they dug tunnels," Platte acknowledged. Bracken picked up the Atlas again and studied it for several moments. Finally, he extended the atlas to Kate.

"Show me where Dr. Rashid was going the night he disappeared." She paused, looking at the Atlas, and finally pointed to a spot inside the penciled circle Platte had drawn the day before.

"Around here, at least that's where he said he was going," she told him. Bracken laid the atlas down so Platte could read it from the other side of the table.

"You said the test and calibration shots you made," he said to Platte, putting his hand on the charts on the left side of the table, "were done here." He pointed to the same-penciled circle. Platte nodded his agreement.

"So, what do you think?" Bracken asked Platte.

"It's gotta be somewhere over here," Platte told him, pointing to the charts Jake was still resting his hand on.

"That's what I thought, too," Jake said, nodding in agreement.

"What's got to be over there?" Kate demanded in confusion and frustration, feeling like she had come in on the middle of the conversation, even though she knew she'd been standing there the whole time.

"The entrance to the tunnel," Platte said picking up one of the beer bottles that were still serving as a paperweight for the charts. He held it up for Bracken to see. "You got any of these that are cold?"

CHAPTER NINE

In Transit – Dallas, TX to Luxor Governorate, Egypt

Jake, Leon, and Kate flew business class from DFW Airport to London Heathrow on American Airlines. When Kate asked Platte why they hadn't just flown one of the planes in Solaris' fleet he had actually answered her in a pretty straightforward manner.

"Crew rest," he had told her. "We can't legally fly non-stop to England from the United States, much less all the way from DFW. We either have to fly a roundabout route via Greenland with a rest and fuel layover, or we have to carry another full crew."

Before leaving his house, Jake pulled Kate aside and asked her an odd question.

"Do you have a cat?" Jake asked her. She was surprised by his question and blurted out the answer without thinking.

"No, I don't. I travel too much," she told him. "Why would you think I have a cat?'

"You look like a cat person," Jake told her with a wry smile.

"And just what does a cat person look like?" she demanded. Her question was answered from the depths of Jake's refrigerator, wherein Leon had poked his head, looking for cold beer.

"Like you," he said, emerging from the refrigerator with a beer in each hand. "Worried about the environment, wanting to make a difference, and thinking cats could actually love a human being beyond our ability to operate a can opener," he said, handing a beer to Jake.

"And what makes you such an expert?" she asked, shifting to face Leon. Jake answered this time.

"Because he's got a cat."

"It's the closest thing to a perfect relationship I've ever had in my life," Leon said, taking up his own story as he opened his beer. "We have an arrangement. I work days, she works nights, we get along."

She started to wade in on the discussion when Jake held up his hand.

"I only asked because I wanted to know if you'd have to board a pet or ask someone to take care of it."

"And why should that matter?" she demanded albeit with less annoyance.

"Because I don't want you to tell anyone you're leaving, which means that if you had to make arrangements for a pet, someone would then know you're leaving, and I would rather keep our departure under wraps," Jake preempted more questions by reminding her of what had happened before.

"Remember someone knew we were going to Paris. "That triggered her memories of her ordeal in Paris, and she looked at Jake, and nodded her renewed understanding.

"Besides," Leon said tossing his now-empty beer can at Jake's kitchen trash. "Cats are very sneaky. First thing you know your exodus is all over Facebook." Kate looked at him without any idea how she should respond to what he said. He returned her attention with a wink.

After clearing customs at London's Heathrow Airport, they were met by a Solaris car and were taken east on the A4 to London City Airport, and then directly to a small Beechcraft King Air B200gt twin-engine turboprop airplane, painted in the Solaris colors.

"Solaris having cutbacks?" Kate asked, looking at the plane. Jake gave her a quizzical look. "No jet this time?" she asked, with a smile. He laughed as he caught her joke.

"I can't get a jet onto the dirt runway at the dig site," he told her as he loaded their luggage. "While this won't be as fast, I can go directly from here to there with just one stop for fuel in Greece." She nodded her understanding.

"It also allows us," he said to her motioning for her to precede him up the stairs into the aircraft, "to file a flight plan to Greece. I won't have to file a flight plan to Egypt until we leave Greece, and if I can get away with it, I won't do that until we're airborne."

"Don't you think you're taking this cloak and dagger stuff a little too far?" She asked, with a chuckle. Jake turned around to face her from the cockpit door.

"Well, if you believe that, I'll save myself some trouble and file a flight plan straight to the dig site," he told her with a very sharp edge in his voice. He held her gaze until she shook her head no.

Her eyes followed him into the cockpit, where Platte was already seated and flipping switches. Although the cockpit looked roomy enough for the two pilots it did not have a navigator's station like the DC3. Therefore, she entered the passenger cabin and seated herself in one of the four-seat lounge areas towards the front of the aircraft.

She had just pulled on her seatbelt when the port engine smoothly came to life. Within a few minutes, both engines were up and running, and the plane taxied to the active runway. The plane idled at the threshold for a few minutes before it moved again, turning right, sprinted down the runway and quickly became airborne.

During the climb out, she watched London dwindle out of the window as the aircraft continued to gain altitude and made several turns. Once the air traffic control ballet of leaving London's active and busy airspace was concluded, the plane turned once more into their final heading.

As the plane climbed to it's cruising altitude Kate closed her eyes and drifted off to sleep. She awoke sometime later and looked out the window to find nothing much had changed. She stretched, unbuckled her seatbelt, and proceeded to the forward part of the cabin, until she stopped when she found a small, but modern galley.

Wondering if she could figure out how to make a pot of coffee, she caught sight of the gallon-sized industrial thermos that was securely strapped onto one of the small galley work areas. She quickly searched for and found coffee mugs and set them on the galley counter. She then filled three mugs about three-quarters full and reached to her left and knocked on the cockpit door.

Someone inside said, "Come," loud enough for her to hear but not to discern who had said it. She opened the door and reached back for two of the mugs.

"I thought you fellas might like a sip," she said, as she handed a mug to each of them.

"Half my kingdom is yours, my lass," Platte cooed, with a mock British accent, as he sipped from the mug.

"Don't let him con you," Bracken said, sipping from his own mug. "He owes money on all of it."

"Actually," Platte said taking another sip, "that's not entirely true. The cat currently holds the mortgage; apparently I'm not a very good poker player." He paused, warming to the subject. "Although I know the little bastard cheats; I'm just not sure where she hides those other aces." Kate couldn't think of an apropos reply, so she just reached for the third mug as she stood in the cockpit doorway.

"How much longer?" she asked, scanning the instrument panel.

"We'll start our descent into Trikala in about 20 minutes," looking at the instrument panel, he added, "we're just now crossing from Macedonia into Greece."

At length, Bracken handed her his now-empty mug, pulled the microphone attached to his headset closer to his mouth, and called air traffic control. He spoke the plane's identification and altitude. He listened for a moment then requested land instructions. Platte handed his empty mug back to Kate after downing the last of the coffee is a large swig.

Understanding they were about to start descending into Trikala, Kate closed the cockpit door, rinsed the coffee cups, and made sure that they were securely stowed. She then returned to her seat and buckled herself back in.

She knew the plane was descending towards the ground, but as she looked out the window, she felt as though the ground was rushing up to meet the plane. The aircraft touched down, taxied off the active runway, and threaded its way to a cluster of hangars on the east side of the terminal.

As the plane slowed, Platte emerged from the cockpit and waited by the exterior door. As soon as the plane stopped, but before the port engine had ceased wind milling, someone outside banged on the door. Platte opened the door but didn't extend the stairs. A man poked his head in the door and said something to Platte.

Leon shook his head and motioned no with his hand. Satisfied, the man retreated from the open door, only to be replaced by another. Leon said nothing to the new arrival but handed him what looked like a credit card. Kate watched out her window, as the second man went to a fuel truck parked nearby and began dragging a hose to their plane.

"We agreed not to leave the plane," Platte explained when they made eye contact. "That way, we don't have to stand for immigration and customs," he told her, leaning out the door to watch the man attaching grounding cables to a nearby tie-down, before connecting the fuel hose.

From landing to takeoff, no more than 45 minutes had passed. Most of that time was spent taxiing to and from the refueling area.

This time, neither pilot closed the cockpit door. As he had told her, Kate heard Bracken call Trikala air traffic control and close out his flight plan to Cairo International, he immediately amended it to an undeveloped strip identifying it's location by latitude and longitude co-ordinance.

Kate turned her attention to the collection of maps and sounding records the three of them had been looking at the night before. Quickly becoming engrossed, she tried to visualize the areas that were represented on the documents she was looking at. She was startled when she heard the pitch of the props change and she felt the plane slow and began to descend. As she stowed her things away, Bracken called to her from the cockpit.

“We're gonna be under ten thousand feet shortly. I'm not sure if you can, but how about trying to call someone at your camp to come get us?” Kate told him she would try.

She powered up her phone and after a few seconds, it showed she had a signal. She placed a call to one of the undergrad students and made a request that someone commandeer one of the battered pick-up trucks and meet the plane at the runway.

Kate felt the plane turn on its final descent and the shudder as the landing gear was extended. She smiled to herself when she saw one of the camp trucks driving into the area by the runway. Once they were on the ground, Platte loaded the truck with their luggage while Bracken performed the usual tasks required at the end of their trip from London.

At long last, they all piled into the back of the ramshackle pick-up for the short ride to the tent compound scattered around the dig site.

After Bracken and Platte dumped their well-traveled duffle bags into one of the empty four-man tents, they met Kate in the dining tent. Taking soft drinks from a cooler, they gathered at an empty table well out of earshot from the other small knots of folks in the dining tent.

Kate heard Platte mumbling something under his breath about Muslim countries prohibition against alcohol. If Bracken heard Platte, he didn't acknowledge it, as he took a long swig from his soda can.

"Well, we're here. Now what?" Platte asked, after taking a drink from his own can and letting out a sigh.

"First thing I think we should do," Bracken said, looking around to make sure no one was listening, "is get some rest. We're eight time zones away from the last time we slept. We're not going to be able to think straight without sleep." Platte and Kate nodded their agreement with Bracken's wisdom.

"Tomorrow," Bracken said looking straight at Kate, "you need to establish a reason for our being here," he told her pointing to first Platte, then to himself.

"Got any suggestions?" she asked.

"As a matter of fact, I do," he smiled. "It allows us to kill two birds with one stone. You need to let the word circulate that you took some of the last week's readings from the GPR back to Solaris. You were concerned over the fact the equipment sat dormant during the recent series of work stoppages and investigations. You don't think the readings are still accurate, so you've asked for Platte to come back and recalibrate the system." He paused and let that sink in.

"That certainly gives me a reason for being gone," Kate said after a moment's thought.

"And," Platte said, picking up the story, "not only does it give us a reason for being here," he said smiling, "it gives me a reason to shoot soundings around where we spotted the tunnels, since that's where I did the calibrations the first time around."

"You do catch on quickly," Bracken said, grinning at Platte.

"Devious people always recognize a devious plan when we hear one," Platte replied, glancing at his now-empty can of soda, "even without the benefit of alcohol."

"And what are you going to be doing?" Kate asked Bracken, as he downed the last of his can's contents.

"I'm going to talk to the laborers," Bracken said, smiling, as he looked around one more time. "I wanna find out about ancient Egyptian mummies, tombs, and more importantly, curses."

CHAPTER TEN

Valley of The Kings – Luxor Governorate, Egypt

Bracken got up before the dawn. He dressed, gathered his smoking paraphernalia, and headed for one of the small fires burning, as the diggers brewed tea and got ready for the day's work. In a repeat of his last visit to the dig site, the workers made a place for him around their fire and gave him tea when it was finished brewing.

While Bracken spoke little Farsi or Arabic, he felt a sense of heightened apprehension among the men crouched around the fire. Their hurried conversations were conducted in muted tones and were accompanied by continued frequent and furtive glances towards the digging areas. Even to a casual observer, something was troubling this group of grown men.

He corroborated this as he wandered in and out of the dig areas, listening and observing. It seemed to him that workers were looking over their shoulders with almost every shovel or wheelbarrow of sand, rocks, and dirt they moved.

At the midday meal, he made his way through the line in the mess tent and was served a plate of rice, beans, and bread. He saw Platte and Kate sitting at one of the tables examining the laptop. Instead of joining them, he chose to sit with one of the small groups of men gathered at another table.

These men were the foremen of the dig sites a few of the Egyptian government officials tasked with safeguarding the heritage of Egypt. Most of them spoke passable English, and some of them recognized Bracken from his previous visit.

For those he did not know he introduced himself as the Solaris pilot who had returned Dr. Compton and Mr. Platte to the dig site, recounting the story Platte, Kate, and he had agreed on the night before.

Bracken listened closely to the conversation, as he had earlier with the diggers. In deference to Bracken, most of it was spoken in English. While no one made direct reference to the disappearances that had occurred in the previous weeks, the incidents hung heavy, but unspoken over the group. Once again Bracken picked up anxiety and concern in and among this group. After finishing his lunch, Bracken sipped his coffee and waited for a lull in the conversation.

"I understand from Dr. Compton that some unfortunate and regrettable trouble occurred here since I was here last," Bracken said, making an effort to as casual as possible.

The gathering of men looked back and forth between each other before one of the gentlemen who had introduced himself to Bracken as Dr. Omeed, an Egyptian government official, replied.

"We have been plagued by several very mysterious deaths and disappearances," Dr. Omeed said, looking down at his empty tray. Bracken silently noted that Dr. Omeed had used the word plagued.

"That's most unfortunate, and I was very sorry to hear about it. Is this a normal occurrence for this kind of dig?" Bracken asked, speaking directly to Dr. Omeed. Dr. Omeed's eyes questioned the others at the table before continuing.

"Accidents happen at all archeological digs. The day laborers are the most frequently exposed to such dangers, but these accidents rarely result in death," Dr. Omeed looked to the other men sitting in the group before resuming.

"However, that is not what has happened here. People have died for no explainable reason, certainly not from a cave-in, or accident from using the equipment." Dr. Omeed said looking into his tea. "Doctor Mohammad died when you were last here, then several of the day workers as well. Also, people who know the deserts and their ways do not wander off into it and vanish. It is most unusual indeed." He stopped and looked around the table again.

"I'm not a man given to superstition, nor are most other educated men," Bracken said, indicating those seated around him. "However, I was raised in America where curses attached to tombs of the departed were standard fare for the Saturday afternoon matinée movies I watched as a boy." Dr. Omeed looked up sharply at him.

"I can assure you that no such reality of that Egypt ever existed anywhere but your movies," he said in a sharp tone.

"Forgive me, Dr. Omeed. I meant no disrespect to you or your colleagues," Bracken replied, holding his hands up in a sign of surrender. "I was merely observing that a
less-educated man could easily go down that path of reasoning."

Dr. Omeed started to retort, but quickly stopped himself when he noticed concerned glances coming from the others. One of them leaned across the table and spoke in a subdued voice, just loud enough for those around him to hear.

"Sidi Bracken," the man said, using a title of respect, "we understand there are no curses other than in name. However, the day workers are not easily convinced of this. With the troubles we've had, you're not the only one to take into consideration the superstition of curses associated with reclaiming our heritage. Many workers have already left due to their fear, and it is becoming difficult for us to find and retain willing workers for our dig."

"We must ask you not to share your memories of your movies with others," he said, as the rest of the group nodded in agreement.

"We have just had a season of bad luck with this project." As if on cue the group rose, en masse to leave the dining tent.

"Allah knows best," Dr. Omeed added. "We are all saddened at the loss of life at any time," he told Bracken as he turned and walked away. Taking his cue from the others, Bracken waited until they had walked towards the exit gathered up his trash and walked out as well.

From the mess tent, Bracken walked directly to the area where Platte was working. Bracken had already heard several of the booms from the mortar blanks Platte had fired from the GPR to create the return signals for the computer to interpolate.

"Any luck?" Bracken asked, handing Platte an unopened bottle of water he had taken from the mess tent.

"I have absolutely no idea," he answered, after taking a long pull from the bottle. "I tried running the data from the computer to Solaris by hot-spotting my phone, but the screen," he told Bracken, holding up his phone, "is too small for me to see any detail." Bracken just nodded his understanding.

"We'll let Kate do it this evening, and see what comes of it," Bracken finally said. "The whole idea," he said, turning to face Platte, "is to look like we're not actually looking for something."

"Got it," Platte said putting his phone back in his pocket. "Sorta like going to a topless beach. Always wear your darkest sunglasses so no one knows you're leering." Platte smiled. "How about you? Find out anything?"

"Nothing directly, but everyone from the diggers to the government guys are jumpy," Bracken replied. "The diggers are more inclined to believe the curse of the Pharaohs is visiting them for some other transgression or directly connected with the dig, while the more educated folks are thinking the same thing, but believe if they don't say it out loud, it isn't true."

"And that way, no one can accuse the brain trust of not being smarter than the diggers, despite all the degrees," Platte said, taking another drink from the plastic bottle.

"Don't you believe in curses, the resurrection, or life after death?" Bracken asked, with a smirk.

"Kid," Platte said, hooking his thumb into his belt and lowering his voice, "I've flown from one side of this galaxy to the other, and I've seen a lot of strange stuff; but I've never seen anything to make me believe there's one all-powerful Force controlling everything. There's no mystical field controlling my destiny."

"That's a pretty decent Obi-Wan Kenobi, you know?" Bracken laughed.

"It wasn't Kenobi, it was Han Solo who said that, and while he might have been wrong about the Force he was right about the other thing." Bracken jerked his head up in a come-on gesture.

"Hokey religions and ancient weapons are no match for a good blaster at your side." Bracken locked eyes with Platte for a moment before nodding and turning to leave.

"And where are you off to?" Platte asked.

"Maintaining my cover as the resident flyboy," he said, over his shoulder. "I'm gonna go take a look at the plane."

Bracken was halfway to the dirt airstrip before he heard another muffled boom, signaling Platte had gone back to work with the GPR.

Once he arrived at the plane, Bracken did a slow walk around, looking for anything dripping from one of the idle engines, or a tire low on air pressure. Satisfied none of these were a problem, he unlocked the plane and hauled himself up into it.

Once inside, Bracken armed the batteries and brought the instrument panel to life. He checked the fuel levels, avionics, electronics, and listened to the radio to makes sure it was working.

Assured that everything in the cockpit was in working order, he went back outside, and busied himself over the next few hours checking oil, hydraulic, and other fluid levels, including opening the fuel tanks and visually confirming what the fuel gauges had told him.

When he had reassured himself, the plane was just as he'd left it the day before, he walked to the door and closed it. He was about to lock it when he recalled his last conversation with Platte. He reopened the door and got back in the plane.

He went into the galley, reached under the cabinet, and felt around for a moment before finding what he was looking for. The sound of Velcro separating filled the galley as Bracken pulled a holstered Glock 9mm pistol from its hiding place.

He left the plane for a second time, this time locking the door and fitting the gun, under his shirt and into the small of his back before heading back to the camp.

As Bracken approached the outer edges of the encampment, the sun was already casting long evening shadows, indicating the end of daylight for another day. Once inside the tent he shared with Platte, he removed the pistol from under his shirt and tucked it beneath the pillow on his cot.

Bracken walked to the group of tents across the compound to what was unofficially known as the women's quarters. He stopped outside Kate Compton's tent and spoke her name. A moment later it was not Kate, but Platte who opened the tent flap and admitted him.

"Is this the meeting of the Egyptian Hemlock Society?" Bracken asked, taking a seat in a cloth chair at the opposite side of a plastic folding table.

"You're not allowed to be funny unless you bring beer," Platte told him, reclaiming his seat.

"Being out in the sun all day makes you cranky," Bracken smiled.

"Being this close to sobriety always makes me cranky," Platte shot back. "There's way too much blood in my alcohol stream."

"Boys," Kate said, trying in vain to suppress a smile, "can we stick to the matter at hand?"

"Yes, teacher," Bracken said, not suppressing his smile as he turned from Kate to face Platte again. "What did we find?" Platte opened the laptop and began moving his finger over the track pad.

"I did manage to find the tunnel," he told them pointing to an image on the screen. "I was operating on the assumption that we are close, if not right on the termination point for it."

"What made you think that?" Bracken asked, with genuine interest.

"From the files you had the Geology Department run from the last soundings, I thought I detected a floor-to-ceiling aspect ratio narrowing of the tunnel starting here," he said pointing to the screen. Then he changed the screen back to the file they were first looking at.

"I picked it up again today," he told them, pointing again to the screen, "in another slice, closer inland than the one in the other file. It is definitely narrowing."

"What does that mean?" Kate asked, looking from one to the other. Bracken motioned with his hand for Platte to answer her.

"More than likely a narrowing means the tunnel is coming to an end and suggests a surface opening."

"Can you extrapolate a location from what you have now?" Bracken asked.

"Maybe, maybe not," Platte told him.

"Why just maybe?" Bracken asked, again with sincere interest.

"Well, unless you are totally sold on Erich von Däniken's hypothesis that aliens in UFOs built the pyramids," Platte began to answer.

"At my age, I'm willing to consider alternative theories," Bracken told him.

"Unless you're willing to buy into that," Platte frowned, indicating he did not appreciate being interrupted, "then the tunnel was dug by hand. This means," he traced his finger along the bottom line of the screen, "the rise will not be consistent or linear. It's going to be hard to calculate definitively." Bracken pulled one of the open maps from the other end of the table beside the computer.

"Show me where this," he nodded to the laptop screen, "is on here." Platte studied the map for a moment and stabbed his finger down.

"Here."

"OK, assuming the UFOs were in the shop that day and they were digging by hand," he smiled at Platte, "what's your best guess as to where the opening is?" Platte's face took on a blank stare as he did calculations in his head.

"Seven hundred to seven hundred-fifty meters west and slightly north of this spot," Platte indicated, putting his finger back on the map. "Assuming, of course, it wasn't Friday afternoon and they didn't rush the job so they could get to happy hour."

Bracken grabbed a pencil lying on the table and traced a line from Platte's finger to the left and drew a small circle. He studied the map for a moment, then straightened up and looked at Kate.

"Does this look familiar?" he asked, using the end of the pencil as a pointer. She looked intently at the map then shook her head. "Let me give you a hint," he told her, sorting through the other maps again. He laid out a new map over the one they'd been looking at. Kate instantly recognized it as the one they had been using in Jake's kitchen. She looked for a moment to orient herself and let out a small gasp.

"That's the area where Dr. Rashid said he was going the night he disappeared," she said, putting her hand over her mouth.

"Bingo," Bracken whispered. He took the map and sat down in his chair letting his eyes trace unseen lines on the paper. After a minute, Kate looked at Platte, who just rolled his eyes and shrugged. After waiting another minute or so Bracken sat back up and laid the map on the table.

"Tomorrow morning, I want you," he pointed at Kate, "to take a jeep and the laptop, and head for town. In the meantime, I'll make noises at breakfast that you and I," he pointed to Platte, "need to go fix something on the plane.

"What am I going to do in town?" she asked.

"You're not going to town," he told her. She gave him a quizzical look. "As soon as you're out of visual range of the camp, circle around and meet us at the plane."

"What are we going to do at the plane?" she asked.

"Yea," Platte chimed in, "what are we going to do at the plane?"

"While I'm making it known that I need your help with the plane," Bracken said, ignoring them both, "you're going to tell the kids you need to run a few more tests tomorrow afternoon, but they should be ready to start back up with the GPR the next morning."

"I'm going to send these files to Solaris tonight and ask Dr. Hauser to get us side view scans with depth indications," he told them.

"You don't have to send the files," Platte spoke up. Bracken raised an eyebrow. "I told you I'd been washing the scans through the hotspot on my phone all day back to Dallas." He pointed to the top of the computer screen that detailed the files location within the Solaris server.

"Even better," Bracken said looking at his watch. "Dr. Hauser should have these in a few hours, and we should have PDFs of the results by the time we get to the plane."

"What are we going to do on the plane?" Kate asked again. Jake paused, considering her question.

"I don't think we have much time to figure this out," Bracken said solemnly. "Everything points to someone either knowing where the entrance is or trying to buy time to figure it out. Either way, we have to assume someone's starting to worry that we're about to find it. That makes them dangerous and desperate."

"Why would anyone be concerned about us discovering an old water tunnel?" She directed her question at both men.

"I don't think it's the tunnel," Bracken said evenly. There was a pause as they waited for him to continue.

"It's the chambers," Platte ejaculated slamming his hand palm open on the table.

"That would be my guess, too," Jake confirmed.

"The chambers? What about them?" Kate asked, still not understanding.

"Stop thinking like a college professor, and start thinking like a dealer in antiquities," Bracken told her. "Specifically, a dealer in rare Egyptian antiquities. If there's anything in those chambers, it has to be five thousand years old or older." She pondered what he was telling her for a moment before her eyes opened wide in astonishment.

"It would be worth a fortune," she said, letting her voice trail off.

"Yes, it would," Bracken nodded in agreement. "So, to answer your twice-asked question, we're going to spend the morning trying to narrow down where Leon is going to scan tomorrow afternoon, in hopes of ascertaining where we can get into the tunnel."

"You know," Platte said, looking at Jake, "it's going to be damn hot in the plane."

"I'll fire up the APU so we can run the air conditioning. I think we're far enough away for anyone will hear us." Bracken said smiling at Platte. "Besides, I'm sure there will be other rewards for your tireless efforts on the plane. Platte looked at him in bewilderment before a wide grin broke onto his face.

"Son of a bitch," Platte slapped Jake on his back, "there's still beer on the plane!"

The morning passed as planned. Bracken and Platte arrived at the plane not long before Kate appeared, driving one of the jeeps. True to his word as soon as Kate arrived Bracken started the APU that provided power to run the air conditioning.

As Jake expected the files had been converted into PDFs and transmitted to him via email from Dr. Hauser at Solaris. As Platte had correctly predicted, the documents from Solaris clearly showed a gradual narrowing of the tunnel as the floor rose to meet the roof, but despite his earlier insinuation, he did not touch the beer until after they'd reviewed the files from Solaris.

"I was giving the APU time to run the refrigerator to cool it down," he informed Kate and Bracken. Bracken winked at Kate assuring her that, while Leon talked a good game, he too wanted his head clear when they reviewed the data.

Using both the maps they already had, and the data emailed from Solaris, they established a more compact area where Platte would start scanning that afternoon.

When they were done, Bracken extended the power stairway for them to exit the plane.

"You," he said, pointing to Kate, "need to go back the same way you came." "You," he said pointing to the beer in each of Leon's hands "need to finish those before you get back to camp." Leon raised one of the open cans in a salute to Bracken.

"We'll meet back up in your tent after it gets dark to see what Leon was able to find."

"What are you planning to do?" she asked.

"Like any good pilot trying to sell the fact he's been working on the plane all morning, I'm taking it up for a test flight," he told them, patting the door of the plane.

"Actually, I'm going to fly to Luxor International and top off the tanks, but I'll fly over our search area and get a bird's eye view of it," he said holding up his cell phone.

Platte was a fair distance down the road towards the camp before he heard the engines of the plane turn over. A few minutes after he arrived at the GPR equipment, he saw the Beechcraft make a low pass overhead.

Bracken flew west for fifteen minutes before turning the plane a hundred eighty degrees and contacting Luxor International for permission and instructions to land. There wasn't much traffic in the inbound pattern, and Bracken had the plane parked and chocked in less than thirty. Getting a fuel truck to his aircraft turned out to be another matter.

It took him a good hour to get the plane fueled and sign the paperwork for the charge. By that time, his stomach reminded him it had been a long time since breakfast, so Jake walked to the operations building and ordered a cheeseburger and fries at the snack bar. When he finished eating, he returned to the plane, started it, and flew back across the Nile, timing his arrival so he would still have enough daylight to conduct a visual flight rules landing, on the unlit field.

By the time he shut the plane down and walked back to the camp, darkness had fallen, and the scattered tents in the compound glowed like so many fireflies. He went to his tent first to grab a jacket, to ward off the falling temperatures of the gathering desert night. He had just zipped it up, when Kate Compton poked her head inside.

"Oh good; you're back," she told him, looking around the tent. "I thought I heard the plane. Is Leon with you?" In a reflexive move, Bracken looked as well.

"No, I haven't seen him since we left the airfield. Did you check the mess tent?"

"Yes, right before I came over here." Bracken paused, trying to think of where else his friend might be. As he did so, alarm bells started ringing in his head.

Without giving it a second thought, Bracken reached under his pillow, grabbed the Glock, and racked the slide. Kate's eyes widened in alarm when she saw him put the gun in his jacket pocket.

"Where did you see him working last?" Bracken demanded of her.

"Where we agreed he would be working. I saw him there about four." He grabbed her by the arm none too gently, he propelled her out of the tent.

"We gotta get there now. Where's the jeep?" She pointed a few feet away, and ran behind him as he dashed to the driver's side and jumped in.

Bracken covered the kilometer and a half at speeds ranging between too fast and terrifying. The headlights first picked up the GPR system, and then a human form lying behind it. There was motion of another human form moving on foot away quickly and out of the range of the jeep's headlights. Bracken was out of the jeep and kneeling by the figure on the ground before Kate could get fully out of the jeep, grabbing a flashlight to take with her.

"It's Leon," he told her. As she illuminated the scene with the flashlight, Jake gently lifted Leon's head with his hands. When he pulled one of his hands away from Leon's head, the flashlight beam clearly showed Bracken's hand was covered with blood.

CHAPTER ELEVEN

Valley of The Kings – Luxor Governorate, Egypt

"Head wounds bleed a lot because there's a lot of blood flow to them," Kate Compton informed Platte as she changed the compress, she was using to slow down the bleeding from the wound on the back of his head. "The cut isn't actually that bad, from what I can see."

"Be grateful you've stayed clean and sober since you've gotten here, or it could've been worse," Bracken said as he entered Kate's tent where she was tending to Platte. "As you said, there's now plenty good red blood in your bloodstream, and not 80 proof thinner." Locating Bracken from the sound of his voice, Platte looked up and raised the middle finger on his right hand.

"Be still," Kate, admonished him, swatting him on the shoulder.

"Did you find anything?"

"Just footprints leading to a set of jeep tracks in the sand," Bracken answered Platte. "And positively no laptop. Tell me what happened."

"I decided I was done for the day, and I'd just unhooked the laptop with the intention of bringing it here," indicating Kate's tent. "Next thing I remember, you're helping me into the jeep and my head was killing me."

"And you're lucky enough to have a headache and still be alive," Kate said, swatting him again on the shoulder, "be still".

Bracken laughed to himself derisively, knowing full well that the attack on Platte had invoked memories of Paris and both events terrified her.

"She's right, you know," Bracken said more as a statement than a question. "I think we interrupted your imminent demise when we drove up. This guy's killed before."

"If you think you can make yet another mark in the Bracken-saves-mommy-Platte's-favorite-son column," Leon said looking up at Jake, "you've got another thing coming."

"You're an only child," Bracken told him matter-of-factly, "and even so I sincerely doubt you're her favorite."

"I still think you need to go to Cairo and be checked for a concussion," Kate said, looking to Bracken for support.

"I told you already, I don't have a concussion," Platte insisted as Kate applied more pressure to his wound. "Ow, that hurts."

"And just how do you know that you don't?" she asked.

"I've had concussions before, and this doesn't feel like that."

"And just what does a concussion feel like?" Kate asked, annoyance evident in her voice.

"Like a tequila hangover without that dead worm taste in your mouth." Despite himself, Bracken laughed out loud. Kate glared at him as Platte continued.

"This is more like a case of beer and a losing football game bet hangover."

"Well," Bracken began, taking a seat across from Platte, "while I'm very grateful your head is still attached to your shoulders, I also wished you were still attached to that laptop."

"Can't we just redo the scans later?" She asked.

"I'm afraid our cover, as they say," Bracken nodded to Platte, "is blown. They know that we know, and that puts all of us in danger."

"Did you call the authorities while you were out?" Kate turned and looked at him. Bracken shook his head to indicate he had not.

"Why not?" She wanted to know.

"So far, we are the only ones who know this happened, if we report it, the cops will shut the dig down again. If that happens, all we're going to find once we discover the entrance is a dry, empty tunnel," Bracken replied introspectively.

"Then what are we going to do?" Kate asked as she applied gentle pressure to the compress.

"A very good question," Bracken answered, as he leaned back in the chair.

"I forgot to turn it off," Platte said from underneath the compress Kate was using.

"It's off," Bracken told him, "I made sure when I went back to look for the laptop."

"Not the GPR," Platte reached for his belt, unclipped his phone and held it up, "this. I still had the phone set up to hot spot the computer. I forgot to turn that function off yesterday. All the data I collected today already went to Solaris," he paused to let that sink in. A smile slowly formed on Bracken's face.

"Then everything you recorded yesterday is on the server in Dallas?" Bracken asked. Platte slowly, and with a great deal of effort, nodded his head. Bracken reached into his shirt pocket, took out his own phone, and began typing on the screen.

"Then I'll have Dr. Hauser pull it, plot it, and send it back to us in a few hours." Platte looked at his watch. Kate noticed he wore it not on the outside but the inside of his arm.

"It's almost one o'clock here that makes it eight in the morning in Dallas. How long before they can get everything back to us?"

"I would guess by six here at the latest," Bracken answered him.

"Oh no you're not," Kate said looking at Bracken. "I can't believe you two," she said in exasperation. "Your buddy here gets whacked on the head, knocked out, and just because he's now sitting upright and talking, you think he's all better."

"He's going to bed. I don't have anything to give him for pain, but I'll canvass the kids from the university, and get him a bottle of his favorite sedative. He's going to self-medicate and go to bed."

"How do you know any of them have booze?" Bracken asked her skeptically. "This is a dry project." Kate gave him a disbelieving look.

"So are the dorms in Dallas," she replied dismissively. Bracken shrugged, granting her the argument. "You're going to get drunk, and then you're going to bed and sleep it off," she declared insistently, looking down at Platte.

"Do you know if your practice is accepting new patients and takes Solaris' insurance?" Platte asked, without looking up. "I like your bedside manner." She replied by swatting him on the shoulder again.

"I do have one small request," Platte entreated.

"What?" she asked, annoyance in her voice again.

"If at all possible, anything but scotch, please. I so do hate scotch." Bracken could see Platte wince as he smiled.

<<<<<<< >>>>>>

Bracken took advantage of Kate Compton's prescription for Platte and slept in himself. It was close to 8:00 a.m. when he quietly got up, dressed, and let himself out of the tent. Before leaving he did walk over and check on his friend.

Despite Platte's reputation and claims, Bracken noticed there were no more than two good drinks missing out of the bottle that had magically appeared fifteen minutes after he got Leon back to their own tent. He checked the sleeping man's pulse and found it slow, steady, and strong.

He made his way to the mess tent and through the serving line, before taking a seat across one of the plastic tables from where Kate was sitting, working on her laptop while she sipped a cup of coffee.

"So, now we're even," he said to her taking a seat as Kate looked up.

"What do you mean?"

"For Paris," he told her, sipping from his own coffee cup. "I appreciate what you did for Leon last night." A blush rose in her cheeks.

"I just happened to be the only one there and available when you left to see what you could find," she waved her hand as she looked back down at the computer, "besides, all I did was patch up his hard head," she said smiling.

"And find booze for him," he added sipping from his cup again.

"And find booze for him," she confirmed. "How is he?"

"Still sleeping. I checked his pulse and it was good," he told her. "He's not going to be fun to live with when he finally does wake up."

"Between the nasty blow on his head and the bourbon I bet he'll have one helluva of a headache," she said, looking up.

"Oh, I'm sure he will; but that's not what I mean," he said, before forking eggs into his mouth. "I'll have to listen to him retell the story of his attack for months, and it will get more melodramatic with each rendition." Kate laughed out loud.

"All joking aside," Bracken said, in between bites, "we'll need to figure out what to do now, when, and how."

"I've actually been giving that some consideration," she told, him lowering her voice.

"I have, too; and I need to go first," he said lowering his voice as well. She nodded her acquiescence. "The question you need to answer first is, why bother?" Kate looked at him, puzzled.

"It's really simple," he began, "you came here to find history, not hidden caverns with swag. You could just let that part go and focus on what you and the kids came here to do."

"Or?" she asked.

"Or, we keep going, find the tunnel entrance, and who knows what else," he said, looking into her eyes. "Which," he continued, "might not be the brightest idea I ever had." She remembered that look from Paris and realized he was genuinely concerned for her. Without thinking, she reached across the table and put her hand on his.

"I'm truly grateful for your concern, but I need to know what happened to Dr. Walker, and why the others have died or disappeared. If, as you suspect, the rooms above the tunnel contain artifacts they belong to the Egyptian people; and not so-well-heeled collectors who don't care how they got what they get."

"If I can prevent that from happening, then I feel like it will be worth the risk," she told him still locked in his gaze. "Jake, I need your help," she said squeezing his hand in hers, "and I understand that now." Bracken returned her squeeze, then removed his hand and blushed.

"OK, that being settled," he told her, clearing his throat, "now we have to figure out where the entrance is and how to get to it."

"And that's what I've been thinking about," she told him. He motioned with his hand for her to continue. "I figure we can at least narrow down where the entrance is located once we analyze the scans from yesterday." Bracken nodded his agreement.

"The problem is the entrance is not going to be just a couple of spades-of-sand, deep. My assumption is that we're going to have to move a lot of earth before we even get close to the entrance."

"I hadn't even considered that," Bracken said to her. "How will we overcome that?"

"That's what I've been thinking about," she told him with excitement in her voice. "The kids from the university that have been here the last six weeks are due to cycle out. Usually, the incoming group is here a couple of weeks before the other group leaves, sort of a time to show-the-newbies-the-ropes. The new group arrived just before we got back."

"OK"

"Well, usually we go through a hands-on course on how to work on an archeological site as part of the incoming group's orientation. It also includes certifying them to use the backhoe."

"A backhoe at an archeological dig?" he asked surprise in his voice.

"Sure, very little of the digging is done with trowels, dental picks, and paintbrushes, like you see on *The Discovery Channel*. Typically, we usually know the first few feet or more is 'modern history' before we get down to the areas of our interest," she looked up with a mischievous twinkle in her eyes, "so we use all kinds of heavy equipment to move the top layers." Understanding began to dawn on Bracken's face brightened with comprehension.

"And it just so happens," Bracken took up the narrative from Kate, "that you'll do your training where the scans show us the entrance might be."

"Exactly."

"Now, I'm really beginning to worry," confounded, she looked at Bracken surprised, "you're hanging around with Platte too much, and you're getting as devious and conniving as he is." She conceded the point with a laugh.

Bracken and Kate spent most of the rest of the morning and afternoon looking over the PDF files Dr. Hauser had sent them from the previous day's scans. Shortly after lunch, Leon joined them, claiming if he was going to sleep any longer, he would need more bourbon.

While he claimed he was feeling no ill effects from either the blow to the head or the alcohol, both of them noticed him moving gingerly as he took a seat at the table and looked at the laptop.

"Just as I suspected," Platte said, after studying the file for about ten minutes. "The digging is uneven." Platte pointed to the screen.

"So," Jake said, looking over his shoulder, "further out than 750 meters?"

"Actually," Platte said, rotating his upper body to avoid turning his head, "no, it's going to be more like 600. They shanked it and increased the angle of ascent."

"Show me here," Bracken said, dragging the flat paper map beside the computer. Platte spent a good five minutes looking back and forth between the computer and the map. Finally, he picked up a pencil and drew a small tight circle.

"Here," he said, "plus or minus five meters is my guess."

"Keeping in mind what you said earlier," Bracken took the pencil from Leon, "that it was trending west and slightly north." He turned the point on the pencil on its side and used it to shade an area on the left.   Leon looked at the area Bracken had shaded and gave him an encouraging thumbs-up.

As promised, the next day Kate had both the departing and incoming groups of students on site teaching them how to use the mechanized digging equipment. Leon joined them and showed the new group how to use and record data from the Ground Penetrating Radar.

Bracken spent most of his day in the mess tent, reading a paperback book and drinking coffee. While reading, he listened to the conversations around him, as groups of people came and went. If anyone thought Kate's activities were unusual, he didn't hear anything about it from the people passing through the mess tent.

Bracken knew whoever had arranged the attack on Leon would be cognizant of what was happening and not fooled by the ruse they were carrying out with the students.

Bracken was keenly interested in who might be keeping tabs on their activities. As best as he could determine, no one seemed to show any interest at all in what was going on.

Platte managed to direct his students to use the GPR in areas close to, or actually in the training field of operation as the groups traded off jobs during the day. Later that night, they reviewed the readings in Kate's tent.

"I have a question," Platte said.

"Which is?" Bracken turned his attention fully to Platte.

"I'm assuming," Platte responded, "that the guy that hit me in the head, isn't waiting on us to find the entrance to this place, and that he already knows where it is."

"At least the general area," Bracken responded. "What's your question?"

"Why hasn't he opened it already?" Leon asked. Kate looked up from the laptop and tilted her head in a physical agreement with Platte that this was indeed a good question.

"Oh, he has," Bracken said, picking up the paper map they'd been looking at the day before.

"How do you know that?" Kate chimed in.

"I don't know it for an absolute fact, I'm just making an educated guess," he told them. "Look," he pointed to the map, "my thinking is this thing runs five kilometers from here to the river. I sincerely doubt they would have created only one entrance at the beginning and one at the end." He let that sink in.

"They would have other openings along the dig." Platte mused out loud.

"Exactly."

"And," Kate took up where Platte had left off, "chances are good some of those openings would be left open to serve as wells. All anyone would have to do is study the historical data from that period to find out where one of those wells was located. There would be plenty of documentation on where to find water for the herds."

"So, why don't we just go find one of those?" Platte asked.

"Well," Bracken began, "first, we'd have to find one. Then there's a matter of logistics, once we'd found it. We would have to move equipment and people to open it, which would lead to a lot of questions we don't want to answer."

"Finally, and most importantly we might run into the guy who hit you in the head," he told them, pointing to Platte.

"I'd like to avoid that at all costs," Platte said tenderly touching the back of his head. He quickly sprang up and exclaimed, "I got it." He looked back and forth between the laptop screen and the map Bracken had been using.

"The terminus is right," he paused, checking the computer once more, "here." His finger landed on the very edge of the area Bracken had shaded the day before.

"How deep?" Bracken asked, looking at the map over Leon's shoulder.

"Looks like about two meters from where we are now," he replied.

"That's still close to six feet," Bracken observed. "I think we need to be closer than that. We need to be able to remove the last bit of cover and do it in all in one night."

"No problem," Kate said, with a grin. "That's one or two scoops with the backhoe. I can get the kids to do it tomorrow, or better yet I can get there before anyone else arrives and do it myself. After that, I can announce that we're moving the whole process to another area, taking everything with us."

"That gets everyone else out of the area as well," she said, folding her arms across her chest.

"That works," Bracken winked at her.

The following morning Bracken heard the backhoe start-up just as he was waking up. He lay in his cot and listened to the metal clank and hydraulics move as Kate scooped two more buckets of earth from the spot Platte was pointing out to her on the map the night before.

She finished in less than five minutes. When she was done, she returned the backhoe into the compound and left it in the staging area with the other heavy equipment.

While she was moving the backhoe, Platte hooked the GPR up to the jeep he had driven them out in and moved it closer to the actual digging location on the other side of the camp. Kate and Platte were both in the mess tent sipping coffee before Bracken, or anyone else, managed to show up for breakfast.

With the help of the departing students, Kate spent her day showing the new arrivals how to dig more carefully with hand tools. Platte cycled groups of four students at a time in and out of his on-site instructional about the use of the GPR.

While everyone else was at the dig site, Bracken wandered the camp gathering items he thought they might need once they had broached the entrance to the tunnel and stored them in his tent. Before the work ended for the day, Bracken loaded everything into a jeep. Then as groups made their way to the mess tent, he drove out of the compound towards the dirt strip where the plane was still parked.

He parked the jeep on the path just behind the first dune he crossed after he was out of the camp. Twenty minutes later, Platte and Kate quietly joined him, and they set out on an indirect path to where they believed the tunnel entrance was located.

Once they arrived, Bracken and Platte retrieved shovels from the jeep, and immediately began digging under Kate's direction and flashlight beam. They'd only been at it for thirty minutes or so when, simultaneously, both their shovels hit stone.

They cleared an area, about three feet square, and were rewarded with a view of stone that had obviously been quarried and placed there by human hands, as opposed to a naturally occurring slab of rock.

"If we're lucky," she told them, "the stone itself is bigger than the actual entrance and was just placed here on top of the opening to seal it. If it's inset and flush, we're going to have a problem getting it out. Find the edges so we can see." The men spent another thirty minutes clearing the stone of dirt and sand. As it turned out they were both lucky and unlucky.

Once they had removed the remaining soil from the stone, they discovered it had indeed been placed on top of and not into the opening. They also found the covering was twelve feet long by eight feet wide and at least four inches thick.

"That's gotta weigh at least two tons, if not more," Platte observed, as he wiped the sweat off his face with the tail of his shirt. "It's laying flat on the ground, how're we gonna move it?" He looked around anticipating confirmation from Bracken. Instead, he heard the jeep start and saw Jake looking over his shoulder as he backed it up to the long edge of the stone. He got out and grabbed a six-foot-long Johnson bar from out of the back of the vehicle.

He handed the pry bar to Platte and walked around the rubble on the ground, finally stopping and picking up a large stone.

"Fifth-grade science class," he said, tossing the stone to the ground by the end of the area they had cleared, "lever and fulcrum."

"Just lifting it isn't going to help us move it though," Kate protested. Platte, who'd experienced years of trusting Bracken, didn't say anything. He positioned the stone and bar in the approximate first half of the stone slab. Bracken got down on his hands and knees as Platte applied downward pressure on the bar.

"Give me a hand," he said to Kate, his voice strained.   She quickly moved to the end of the pry bar behind Platte and added her weight to his. Slowly, as they pushed down, the slab rose about four inches off the ground. "OK, that's as far as she goes," Leon told Bracken.

Jake reached into his jacket pocket and pulled out several round steel balls placing them somewhat evenly between the slab and the ground.

"Done," he told them, as he quickly clambered away. Platte and Kate slowly lowered the slab back down until it was resting on the steel balls. As Platte and Kate caught their breath, Bracken turned to Platte.

"Notice anything when you started lifting that thing?"

"You mean other than you managed, once more to nab the more effortless of the two jobs?" He paused thinking. "Yea, as a matter of fact, I did. No negative air pressure; it was the same as it is out here."

"Which means," Kate said, walking up beside the two, "it's been opened recently. Not here specifically, but the seal has been broken somewhere along the tunnel. Anything that's been sealed up that long, in the heating and cooling cycles of the desert all these years, would have formed a natural vacuum holding the stone fixed to the opening." Bracken just nodded his agreement.

They repeated the process of lifting the stone and inserting the steel balls at the other end of the slab. After they lowered it back down, Bracken took two straps with thick metal "L-Hooks" on the end and tossed them out of the jeep. He then slid the hooks over the edge of the stone furthest away from the jeep and tied the other ends securely into holes in the bumper.

He then got in the jeep, started it, and slowly took up the slack in the straps. Once he was sure the straps wouldn't stretch any more, he slowly feathered the clutch on the jeep and moved it forward. As he did, the stone slab, now resting on the steel balls, slowly and relatively effortlessly, moved behind the jeep, revealing a black void.

By the time Bracken had turned the jeep off and joined them, Kate was on her knees, leaning into the opening, and shining her flashlight into the darkness. After moving the light both left and right, she stood, brushing the sand and dirt off her pants.

"It looks dry," she told them, pointing her light just inside the opening. "I can't see very far back because the angle is awkward," she moved the light back and forth at her feet. "There are steps here, but they're just dirt cut into the side of the rise. I don't know how much weight they'll take."

"I'll go first," Platte, volunteered, "I'm the heaviest."

"OK," Bracken agreed, "you first, then Dr. Compton, then me. I'll bring up the rear. Here," he handed Platte a backpack.

"I hope you put chips in it this time. You know how much I hate carrots," he said, slipping the straps over his shoulders. Bracken laughed and motioned for Platte to get moving. Platte snapped on his light and took three steps down.

"The steps feel solid," he said, over his shoulder, "no handrails or handicapped ramps. I guess these guys were more civilized than we thought. They managed to avoid having to deal with OHSA and the ADA," he told the pair, referring to the government Occupational Health and Safety Administration and the Americans with Disabilities Act. "I can't see very far in front of me, there's a lot of dust in the air."

"I'm coming behind you," Kate called, carefully putting the weight of her left foot on the first step. When she was several steps down, Bracken reached into his backpack and removed the Glock, putting it into the small of his back under his jacket before following her down.

Jake didn't turn on his flashlight, preferring to follow the two ahead of him, while trying to preserve as much of his night vision as he could. When he reached the bottom of the step, he heard a gasp from Kate. He quickened his pace, and came up behind Kate, who had her light pointed off to the left. Platte's light was reflecting off of a white wall with figures painted on it.

"Dead end," Platte said, as Bracken came up behind him. He looked to see why Kate was not pointing her light at the same wall; she was playing the beam of her flashlight over a collection of ancient tools with handles leaning against the wall.

It was obvious these were tools that had been used and left here by the workmen the last time anyone was in this part of the tunnel. There were shovels, pickaxes, and what appeared to be sledgehammers. The handles were all wooden, as were the bills of the shovels. The pickaxes and sledgehammers also featured stones that had been shaped and secured into the end of their handles.

He perused the tools for several moments before turning his attention back to the wall Platte was still shining his light on. The wall had been plastered with white limestone and then annotated with hieroglyphics while the coating was still damp and pliable.

Although some of the limestone coating had fallen from the wall, what remained was almost blindingly white, while the images and writings still maintained their vivid colors.

Kate finally turned her attention and flashlight back to the wall and waved her hand in the air attempting to clear the dust.

"Can you read it?" Bracken asked. She began to say something before Platte broke in.

"Sure," he said, "it says here," moving his finger back and forth over the images without actually touching them, "closed daily noon to one thirty for lunch. Tradesmen's entrance in the rear." Bracken laughed, while Kate scowled at them both. She played her light back and forth for several minutes before speaking.

"It's the name of the overseer, the guy in charge of the project," she looked closer, "and the names of some of the people who worked under him. I think there was a date here once too, but it's gone," she pointed her light at the piles of limestone dust on the floor.

"The last line says something to the effect, 'completed under the wisdom and leadership of Tutankhamun, Pharaoh, Son of Akhenaten, ruler of all Egypt." No one moved while they pondered what she had just said.

"What now?" Platte asked, breaking the reverie. Bracken didn't say anything, but moved closer to the limestone-coated wall, and played his hand back and forth over the areas where the limestone had fallen off, exposing the stones behind it.

They watched as he bent down and gathered some of the fine dust on the floor between his thumb and forefinger. He then moved his hand in front of the exposed areas and let the dust slowly fall from his fingers. Most of it fell slowly back to the floor of the room, but some of it vanished into the cracks of the exposed stones.

"There's a void behind this wall," he advised them, still looking at the stone. Platte immediately moved to a spot beside Bracken and repeated the exercise with the dust from the floor.

"Yep, there is," he turned to Bracken, "now how do we get through to it?"

Bracken didn't say anything but moved a few steps towards the tools leaning against the wall and picked up one of the ancient sledgehammers. As he walked back to where Platte was standing, he tested the soundness of the wooden handle and the tool's weight in his hand.

As soon as he was back in front of the wall, he reared back with the sledgehammer, and prepared to strike the wall.

"STOP," Kate screamed grabbing the tool at the top of its arch behind Bracken. "You can't do that. That wall and that hammer are 4,000 years old or older. You just can't destroy all this," she told him pointing to the wall. "It has to be photographed, cataloged and the blocks marked and removed systematically so they can be reassembled later." As she was pleading with him, Bracken lowered the sledgehammer to the ground while still maintaining a loose hold on the handle.

"This isn't like some mud and rock dam on your ranch. It's priceless ancient history and can't be replaced." As she finished, she placed both her hands defiantly akimbo on her hips. Bracken considered her in the reflection of Platte's flashlight beam for a long moment.

"You're right," he said, looking at her, "I can't." After consenting, he turned to Platte, holding out the sledgehammer. As Platte took it from Bracken's hand, Bracken winked at him.

Platte took the tool from Bracken, and without pausing, reared back and smashed the wall with it.

CHAPTER TWELVE

Valley of the Kings – Luxor Governorate, Egypt

The first blow knocked a lot of the limestone plaster off the wall and dislodged one of the rocks behind the limestone. Before Kate could overcome her shock at what had happened, Platte took another whack at the same spot, causing the loose stone to fall out on the other side with a thud, leaving a gaping black hole.

"I can't believe you did that," she finally managed to spit out. "There's no way any of this," shining her light on the floor, now littered with the limestone plaster, "can be recovered. It's now lost forever."

"Get over it, Doc; we had to get in," Platte told her, before taking yet another swing at the wall, knocking out more stones.

"Look," Bracken entreated, as Leon continued increasing the size of the hole, "I can appreciate your feelings, but we don't have time to wait the three weeks you would need to be the archeologist. We've got to find out what's on the other side and we need to do it now."

Bracken's speech lasted longer than he had planned and when he was done, he looked back at Platte.

Having breached the interlocking structure of the stones in the wall, Leon was now using the head of the ancient sledgehammer to increase the opening, both vertically and horizontally, by easily knocking the stones out of the way.

After he'd created a large enough gap in the wall, he leaned in to have a look. He was only across the barrier for a moment before standing up, taking his flashlight from Bracken's hand, and disappearing into the dark hole.

"Five meters, then it starts down," he called, from the darkness. "The slope looks gradual, and I can't detect any moisture." He paused for a moment, shining his light around into the darkness.

"Ah, Houston, we've got a problem," he announced, shining his light to his right of the opening. Bracken poked his head into the opening and looked where Platte was pointing the beam.

"Yea, I agree," he turned to Kate. "Dr. Rashid or Walker?" Puzzled she brushed past him, and her head through the opening. She let out a gasp and quickly pulled herself back out.

"It's Dr. Rashid," she told him, as she covered her mouth with her hand. Bracken moved closer to her as her other hand moved to her stomach. A moment later, she sprinted to the other side of the room, and Bracken could hear her retching in the darkness.

When she walked back to Bracken, he had already taken a bottle of water out and soaked a handkerchief.

"Here," handing her the handkerchief. She took it without comment, wiping first her mouth then the rest of her face. Bracken walked back to the opening and spoke to Platte.

"How long has he been there?" Bracken asked, in a low voice. Platte knelt by the body and shined his light on the face for a long moment; if being this close to a dead body bothered Platte it didn't show.

"He's somewhere between the gooey and mummy stage of decomp so," Platte paused thinking, "I'd say four to five weeks."

"Any clue how he died?" Bracken wanted to know. Platte shined his light back over the body, and then behind it, back towards the tunnel.

"No," he shined his light on the dirt floor revealing dark spots trailing off down the tunnel, "but he was leaking pretty badly when he got here." Bracken nodded his thanks and pulled his head out of the wall and turned back to Kate.

"I'm sorry about Dr. Rashid," he sympathized. "Can you go on?" Bracken asked he could see the confusion in her eyes; she couldn't decide if she was still mad at him for what Platte had done to the wall or grateful for his concern for her. Kate took a deep breath, gripped her flashlight tighter, and stepped through the opening in the wall. Platte followed the beam of her light, as it pointed straight ahead and disappeared into the tunnel.

Bracken just shrugged and brought up the rear of the procession stepping through the opening to other side. As he did, he heard Kate talking to Leon.

"Why are you bringing that thing with you?" She pointed her flashlight beam at Leon's hands still holding the sledgehammer.

"I've become very attached to it," he replied, looking down at it. "You, of all people, should know how hard it is to find the right tool when you're on an archeological site."

"What you did back there wasn't archeology," she paused trying to find the right word. "It was barbarism," she spat out, to reinforce her disgust.

"One man's barbarism is another man's archeology," he retorted. "It depends, I suppose, on which side of the wall you're standing on, now doesn't it?" When he'd finished she turned and glared at Bracken.

"If looks could kill, old buddy," Platte told him, turning back to the tunnel, "we'd just bury you here." Before Kate or Bracken could respond, Leon pointed his flashlight directly in front of them. The light vanished into the darkness not striking anything anywhere close.

"This thing is huge," they heard Platte proclaim out of the darkness.

"How big do you think?" Bracken inquired.

"Ten meters wide, at least," Leon, responded, panning his light from side to side.

"And I would guess," Kate said, "20 to 30 feet high. Entirely dug by hand," she said in awe. They stood, just looking and taking in the enormity of the cavern before Bracken broke up their reverie.

"We'd better get moving," he said, turning on his flashlight. With that, they all began walking abreast down the incline. They walked for a good ten minutes before reaching level ground.

"How far to the first cavern?" Bracken asked.

"At least two thousand meters from the bottom of the ramp," Platte answered him after mentally calculating what he could remember from the last set of scans.

"A little over a mile and a half," Bracken said, converting the measurements from metrics to mileage. He used his flashlight to motion the group forward. They continued for another ten minutes, before Bracken pulled up short and turned off his flashlight.

"Stop," he said dropping his voice and holding out his arm. "Turn off your lights," he whispered. Platte and Kate doused their lights in compliance with his order.

"What is it?" She asked, echoing Bracken's whisper.

"Smell it?"

"Smell what? She demanded.

"Diesel fumes," Platte said.

"I'd bet," Bracken whispered, "our tomb robbers are using a diesel generator up ahead for lights and ventilation."

"What does that mean?" She wanted to know.

"Well, first but not least of which is we were right; somebody else knew about the tunnel."

"And second?" Platte wanted to know.

"If they're running a generator, that means there are several of those somebodies up ahead."

"If they're using a generator for lights why don't we see them?" Kate asked.

"We're still too far out. I'm just guessing, mind you, but when we opened our end of the tunnel, we created a crosscurrent with the airflow. The fumes traveled on the breeze we made. The light doesn't." No one said anything else for a moment, and then Platte spoke up in a whisper.

"It also means they're almost done emptying the chambers."

"What makes you think that?" Bracken wanted to know.

"It stands to reason," he said, keeping his voice low, "they would've started their evacuation with the chamber closest to where they entered the tunnel. We know from the scans the chamber ahead of us is the first one coming from this end, which also means it the last one coming from the other end."

"Make sense," Bracken agreed.

"So, what now?" Kate wanted to know.

"We're going to wait here another minute and let our eyes adjust to the darkness, then we're going to slowly make our way forward," he told her.

"In the pitch dark?" Kate whispered incredulously.

"Nope," she heard Bracken say, then saw his face light up. "I'll activate the screen on my phone, and that

should give us enough light to see where we're going."
He motioned with his hand for them to continue.

As they walked, Bracken's phone would periodically turn itself off due to inactivity. He would then press the on button again to bring the screen back to life. They'd been walking for about 20 minutes; when they began to detect light further up ahead. As they continued to walk, heard the faint noise of a small diesel engine.

Another five minutes, and the light ahead of them resolved into three separate points of light none of which were pointing directly at them. Bracken powered off his phone and put it in his back pocket.

"What's the play?" Platte asked.

"I'd like to get a little closer to find out what they're doing," Bracken replied. "I don't think they can see us, as long as we stay this side of the light. Slowly and more cautiously, they moved closer to the source of light.

As they did, they were able to hear snatches of conversation, in both English and Arabic. Bracken stopped them again, and squatted on the dirt floor of the tunnel, motioning the others to do the same.

"Now what?" Kate whispered.

"I have absolutely no idea," Bracken muttered.

"What do you mean, you have no idea?" She whispered indignantly. She heard Platte chuckle in the dark.

"You can't write a syllabus for real life," Platte whispered. "We had no idea what was down here, or even if we could get down here."

"Shut up, both of you!" Bracken whispered, as forcefully as he could. "We need to move, one at a time, as slowly and quietly as we can, towards the left side," he told them. "Their lights are arrayed to cover the middle. There are more shadow on the sides."

"Why the left?" She heard Platte groan.

"Because most people are right-handed, which means your peripheral vision favors your left," he answered. If having to explain his reasons annoyed him the other two did not hear it in his voice.

"Then why are we moving to the left?" She wanted to know.

"Our left," Platte whispered; she could hear the grin in his voice, "which means their right, as they look down the tunnel."

"Oh," was her only reply. She felt Bracken reach behind her and tap Platte on the shoulder. He immediately rose, and with meticulous steps, started off to the left.

After a few moments, Bracken gave her shoulder a tap and she followed Platte attempting to duplicate his stealth. There was just enough light for her to make him out, as she reached the side. Bracken joined them 30 seconds later.

"Follow behind me," he instructed. "Move as carefully and quietly as you can."

"Yes, be vehwee, vehwee qui-et, we be hunting wabbits," Platte whispered. Although it was too dark to see, Kate was sure Bracken turned and scowled at Platte.

The closer they got, the more the scene under the lights resolved. A very long, sturdy, aluminum ladder extended from the floor of the tunnel and vanished up into the roof. A man was standing about a third of the way up on the visible portion of the ladder, and occasionally reached up to receive an item that was handed down to him. In turn he handed the item down to another man, standing at the foot of the ladder who placed it in a trailer, which was hooked to the back of small four-wheeled vehicle similar to, but smaller than the one she had seen Bracken driving on his ranch.

As they continued to inch forward, and the light improved, Kate saw Bracken reach under his jacket and remove the Glock.

"Keep her here," Bracken told Platte, then increased his stride and walked into the light, where he became fully visible to everyone in the tunnel. As he did so he smoothly racked the slide on the pistol.

"Hi, guys," Bracken broadcasted, leveling the pistol at the two men he could see. "Tell your buddy upstairs to come down slowly, and to make sure I can see both his hands on the ladder." The two men just stared opened mouthed at Bracken.

"I know you speak English," he said, "but just in case, let me translate it into a universal language everyone speaks." With that, he racked the slide on the pistol. Immediately, the man on the ladder looked up and spoke something in Arabic, before starting down the ladder. As he reached the ground, another pair of legs appeared at the top and began to descend.

As the third man stepped onto the floor of the tunnel, Bracken thought he heard Platte grunt, and then a loud thud behind him. The sound of Kate screaming quickly followed.

As Bracken twisted around to see what was happening, a voice, he thought he recognized, wafted from deeper in the shadow of the tunnel.

"Ah, Mr. Bracken, we've been expecting you," he heard midway through his turn towards Kate. He could almost place the voice now, but before his brain could register its identity, the darkness of the tunnel closed in on Bracken's consciousness.

CHAPTER THIRTEEN

Valley of the Kings – Luxor Governorate, Egypt

Bracken knew exactly where he was when he regained consciousness. He also quickly surmised he was sitting on the floor of the tunnel his hands were bound behind him with a zip tie, separated by the pole holding up one of the portable lights. What he did not know was where the cool moist feeling on his neck was coming from. Blood, as a general rule, was warm and sticky.

He slowly opened his eyes to resolve the question, and found Kate kneeling beside him, applying a small hand towel soaked in water to the be back of his neck. There was an undeniable look of relief on her face when he opened his eyes.

"Welcome back," she greeted him with a brave smile.

"Where's Platte?"

"I'm right here," he heard over his shoulder.

"You OK?" Bracken wanted to know. He realized that he was sitting with his back against Leon's. Kate answered for him.

"He seems to be but it's hard to tell with him. I asked him his name and where he was and who the president of the US was. He did fine, right up until the president question," she said while parting the hair on the back of Bracken's head to look at his wound. "Who's Alfred E. Neuman?" Bracken chuckled and immediately regretted it because his head moved.

"I really wish people would quit hitting me in the head," Platte interrupted, "my barber's not that careful cutting hair back there."

"This is my first time, and I hope not to repeat it," Bracken told him. "Do you know what's going on?"

"No," he replied. "I was out until just before you came to."

"How long was that?"

"Ten or Fifteen minutes," Kate told him.

"Who hit us?" Bracken wanted to know.

"I did," a voice answered, from behind Bracken. Bracken slowly turned this head towards the source of the voice.

"I ascertained from where you've been working," he continued, looking at Kate, "that you'd found a way into the tunnel. Even with the generator running, you'd be amazed at what an echo chamber this place is. We heard you coming through the wall at the end of the shaft."

Despite their predicament, Kate glared at Bracken and Platte.

"Oops," Platte mumbled.

"Dr. Walker," Bracken interjected, finally connecting the voice with his memory.

"You don't seem surprised to see me," Dr. Walker said, moving into Bracken's line of sight.

"I had all but narrowed it down to either you or Dr. Rashid," Bracken told him soberly. "Once we entered the tunnel and found Dr. Rashid dead, it sorta left you as number one bad guy."

"Poor Omar," Dr. Walker lamented, referring to Dr. Rashid by his first name. "He spotted the tunnel in the first sets of scans he saw after he took over from Dr. Mohammad," he casually informed Bracken. "He got very excited. I tried to convince him that it was just an anomaly of the equipment, but he knew of the irrigation tunnel legends too."

"Seeing no other choice, I eventually agreed with him that the anomalies could actually be evidence of an ancient tunnel. I told him that was why I'd sent Ms. Compton to Paris. I was hoping to stall him long enough to take care of things here before he caught on to what I was doing."

"Sadly," Dr. Walker shook his head, "he followed me to our entrance and down in the tunnel one night. He had some misguided old-school ideas about what should be done with the artifacts we found. We had," he paused for a moment to think, "philosophical differences about who should benefit from my discovery. Just out of curiosity, where did you find him?"

"He made it all the way to the other end," Bracken nodded in the direction they'd come from.

"A pity," Dr. Walker said, tilting his head. "After Dr. Mohammad died, Omar saw this as his big chance for promotion and glory. I do regret having to shoot him."

"Can I assume you killed Dr. Mohammad as well?" Bracken wanted to know.

"Of course, I did," Dr. Walker smiled. "You see, he also spotted the tunnel in the scans. It would seem his knowledge of the legends was more complete than Omar's. When he saw the caverns above the tunnel on the scans, he immediately understood their significance as well."

"And just what is their significance?" Kate asked entering the conversation.

"Haven't you already figured it out?" He wanted to know, speaking directly to Kate in a mocking tone of voice. "One of my best and brightest, and you can't guess what they are?" When she did not reply, he continued his diatribe.

"They are storage chambers, of course," he said, addressing all three of them.

"Most people presume the history of the Pharaohs transpired in a somewhat orderly succession of dominion and authority being passed from one ruler to his appointed heir," he told them, adopting on the manner he would use to address a class of undergraduates. "It was never that way, of course. Egyptian history is rife with the usual skullduggery, backstabbing and palace intrigue that seems to permeate every civilization in Africa, then and now."

"There was always someone, either within or outside of the family, willing to dethrone one Pharaoh in favor of another, or most cases, themselves," he pontificated, clearly relishing his role as the resident expert. "And that just addresses the internal strife. Egypt's history is also a chronicle of threats from external forces as well; Hittites, Nubians, as well as the Upper or Lower Kingdoms, to name just a few. "

"So," he continued, "from time to time, the ruling Pharaoh, feeling threatened by one faction or another thought it a good idea to hide the treasures of his kingdom."

"And what better hiding repository could he contrive than the old irrigation tunnel that no one even remembered existed," he swept his hand around him, to indicate where he stood. "Dig chambers above the tunnel, stash your loot, seal the chambers, then flood the tunnel and voilà: you have the perfect hiding place. After the threat passes, dam up the tunnel, wait for it to drain, and reclaim your treasure."

"Speaking of undiscovered secrets," Bracken interjected, "how exactly did you kill Dr. Mohammad?"

"A simple method really," he smiled. "Once he was asleep, I took a large bore needle and injected him with several hundred ccs of air, which created a pulmonary embolism and stopped his heart"

"Then why didn't the injection site get spotted in the autopsy?" Bracken asked.

"Ah, that's where I took a risk, albeit a small one, but a risk nonetheless," he explained. "I injected him just under a mole on his arm. The mole masked the discoloration from the injection. But I needn't have worried; you see, Dr. Mohammad was not a very devoted Muslim. He drank a great deal, and the overworked doctor in the Cairo morgue just assumed it was the alcohol finally demanding its due."

"And I suppose that's when you planted the ole' curse story?" Platte asked.

"My dear young man," Dr. Walker laughed. "Someone's curse looms over every archeological dig from Navajo burial sites in New Mexico to the interior of China. This place," he swept his hand around him again, "is no different. In fact, it's assumed every spade of dirt or sand turned over in Egypt pisses off some deity or other and brings down a curse. The curse scare was completely unplanned on my part, but not at all unwelcomed."

"Did you hear that?" Platte bumped his back against Bracken's. "He called me a young man."

"It's pretty dark in here," Bracken replied. "He really can't see well." Then, under his voice, so only Platte could hear, he said, "Keep him talking so I can look around."

"Is that why you killed the two diggers, to fuel the curse chatter?" Platte continued, as Bracken had asked.

"Again, it didn't hurt my cause, but I didn't kill haphazardly," he said tersely. "Unfortunately, Omar," he paused and corrected himself, "Dr. Rashid had asked them to recount the legends of watering wells between here and the river; I had no choice but to stop them from talking." Platte was about to ask something else when Bracken moaned and fell onto his side.

Kate, who'd been standing not far from them quickly knelt and leaned over Jake.

"I'm ok," he told her, under his breath, once he was sure she was blocking Dr. Walker's view. "I need you to do something. I need you to get me one of the flashlights in the backpack, and then somehow get it over to us. Can you do that?"

"Maybe, but why?"

"Kate, I don't I have time to explain; just do it please," Kate bobbed her head slightly to let him know she understood. She helped pull him upright, but noticed that he had shifted in the process, so that neither his nor Platte's hands were visible. She stood and started towards one of the backpacks that lay a few feet away.

"Ms. Compton," Dr. Walker said. She looked up and noticed he was now holding Jake's pistol. "Where are you going?"

"To get some water for him," she replied, nodding towards the backpacks.

"How kind of you. Tell you what. You unzip the backpack, then grab it by the bottom and dump it out on the ground." She did as instructed. She scattered everything between her legs where she was kneeling. In the emptied contents were two full bottles of water. Without looking back, she picked up one of the bottles and walked back to where Platte and Bracken were sitting.

She uncapped the bottle, breaking the seal, and held it up for Bracken to drink from, while Dr. Walker looked over her shoulder.

"Thanks," he told her, after he'd finished drinking. "I guess I'm still a little light-headed," he said loud enough that everyone could hear him. Kate moved to Platte and gave him a drink as well.

"Sorry," she told him, as she screwed the cap back on the bottle when he had finished, "it's just water." She smiled uneasily at him.

"It's ok, darlin'," he said, mocking a Texas drawl, "you done good." When she stood up, she looked back towards the opening in the ceiling.

"May I?" she asked Dr. Walker, pointing to the trailer.

"Of course, by all means, please do," he told her waving the pistol in the direction she'd indicated. As she approached the trailer, the three men who they'd seen when they first arrived, moved back in obedience to a command spoken in Arabic by Dr. Walker.

"Hey," Bracken whispered, as soon as the pair was out of earshot.

"Yea," Platte whispered back.

"Look at the lights and tell me if you think they're hooked up series or parallel," he said, leaning towards the light stand they were zip-tied to. Platte shifted a little to get a better look; after a moment he whispered back.

"Series," he told Bracken.

"So, if we can get one of the lights to go out," Bracken mused, "they'll all go out."

"Good plan, just one problem," Platte whispered, "if all those lights go out, we can't see either."

"I still have my phone," Bracken told him.

"I think," Platte said, "we're gonna need to see sooner than Amazon can get flashlights here. That's all based of course on the rather unfounded belief that you can get a signal down here so you can place the order."

"Whatever we do, I have a feeling we need to do it sooner rather than later," Platte nodded his agreement, though Bracken couldn't see it.

"May I take this over and look at it in the light?" they heard Kate asking as she picked up something from the trailer. Once more Dr. Walker granted her passage by motioning with Bracken's pistol. She walked directly to the light pole Bracken and Platte were attached to, holding up a jewel-encrusted medallion to the light.

"The nineteenth dynasty?" She asked, over her shoulder, turning the piece over in her hands.

"Twentieth, actually," he corrected her, "Sety-nekht to be precise."

"I'm sure you're right,' she told him solicitously. "It's exquisite, regardless." She turned and held it back up to the light. As she did, Bracken and Platte heard her exclaim "Oh shit!" as the medallion slipped out of her hands and on to the sand on the tunnel floor.

Immediately, she dropped to her knees to pick it up. With her back to Dr. Walker, and with her left arm extended to pick up the medallion she dropped, she let something slide out of the sleeve of her jacket; moving as quickly as she could to hide it in the sand behind where Bracken was leaning against Platte.

"Do be more careful," Dr. Walker admonished, her as she retrieved the piece and stood back up. "It is, after all, rather priceless." He chuckled at his own joke.

As she walked back towards the trailer Bracken probed into the sand to retrieve what Kate had buried. Once he grasped and identified it he bumped his back against Platte again.

"Well, we've got the light thing solved," he whispered. "She palmed one of the flashlights out of the backpack when she got the water."

"I'll have to stake her the next time I play poker with the cat," Platte whispered back. "I might even be able to get the mortgage back."

"You live in an apartment."

"Minor technicality," Platte told him. "Do you know what the Boy Scout definition of a flashlight is?"

"No, what?" he asked.

"A storage container for transporting dead batteries," Platte answered morosely.

"I sincerely hope that's not the case here," he said, putting the flashlight into Platte's hand by feel. "Twist it and break my zip-tie, then I'll do yours." As Bracken watched Kate walk away, Dr. Walker blocked her path.

"As I said before," he looked at Kate, "you were without a doubt one of my best and brightest protégés." As he spoke, his free hand traveled up and he traced his finger inside the opening of her blouse. "And you're not without other noticeable attributes as well," Dr. Walker said peering down at her shirt, that was concealing her breasts.

She immediately jerked back from his touch leaving his hand hovering in midair. As she did, the three men behind Dr. Walker laughed in understanding as to the meaning of both his words and gesture. Dr. Walker sighed.

"Too bad," he said looking back into her face, "you would have been interesting company. Oh, well," he shrugged coming to a conclusion, "you do know that you will die with your friends?" he asked, motioning towards Bracken and Platte.

"You would shoot three more people in cold blood? For what?" She demanded. "To get rich by selling ancient treasure from the Pharaohs," as she spoke, she flung the medallion, and hit him in the chest. He just laughed at her.

"Shoot you? No," he told her, turning the gun over in his hand. "And kill you over a few antiquities; certainly not. Selling this stuff," he moved his head, indicating the trailer behind him "is just a means to my end." He bent down and picked up the medallion.

"Compared to what I have in mind, this stuff," he held up the medallion, "is mere pocket change." She looked at him with a totally baffled look on her face.

"If not for the artifacts, then what?"

"Oil, my dear Dr. Compton. The blackest of all gold."

CHAPTER FOURTEEN

Valley of the Kings – Luxor Governorate, Egypt

"There are no significant oil reserves in Egypt," Platte said, as a knee-jerk reaction, "the geography and geology are all wrong."

"So I've been told," Dr. Walker responded to Platte, "by everyone who knows anything about it.   In point of fact, did you know that Norway has more known oil reserves than Egypt? Egypt's reserves are on par with," he paused that thought a moment, "Vietnam." When Platte did not comment further, he turned back to Kate.

"You really don't want to do that again," Bracken whispered. "We don't want anyone looking over in this direction now, do we?"

"Sorry," Platte confessed. "I just hate being subjected to stupidity and not pointing it out. I'm the same way during the election seasons at home."

"Well, put a cork in it for now." Bracken told him. He looked over at the two Egyptologists as Dr. Walker resumed his explanation. Kate was looking at him, and he directed her, with his eyes, to turn back and listen; at the same time, he hoped she understood he wanted her to keep Dr. Walker's attention away from where he and Leon were sitting.

"You see," Dr. Walker continued, once he had regained Kate's full attention, "about five years ago I was doing some research. I needed to round up another expedition, so I was looking for a promising opportunity when I happen upon some documents from the time when Horemheb was Pharaoh." Dr. Walker paused, refreshing his memory.

"Horemheb was the head of both Tutankhamun's and Ay's armies. Ay replaced the boy king upon his untimely death. The widely accepted belief is that Horemheb, was Nefertiti's lover, and through Horemheb, she controlled Egypt during both Tutankhamun and Ay's short reigns. Unlike you, my dear, Nefertiti was a rather ambitious bitch," he chuckled at Kate's visible discomfort.

"At some point, Horemheb, or more than likely Nefertiti, tired of being in the background, usurped the throne, by force, from Ay. It all gets very convoluted," he told her, waving his free hand as if to dismiss the serpentine genealogy.

"Anyway," he said leaning against one of the light poles, "there I was, looking for something that I could write a grant for and I stumbled upon documents in the archives that were written by Nefertiti herself to Horemheb, making reference to a new power the priest had discovered that would 'light up the night sky and make it as day in the depths of the city of Thebes'. Or so she had written. This was during the reign of her stepson Tutankhamun. And I, of course, was now curious about this discovery."

He paused his lecture, turned to the men standing behind him, and issued a short command. Immediately, one of them started back up the ladder, and the others shifted to where they had been when Bracken had interrupted them. Satisfied his orders were being obeyed; he turned back to Kate, with a look of contemplation.

Fearing things were moving too quickly to a conclusion; she glanced back over to Bracken and Platte. Bracken once again motioned with his eyes that she should continue to keep Dr. Walker talking.

"And where did your research take you next?" She asked, earnestly trying to restart the conversation.

"What?" he asked. "Oh, yes. Well, I went on a quest, as it were, to find as much correspondence between Nefertiti and Horemheb, while still searching for other references to this new source of power."

"That part of the research was easier than the love notes between Nefertiti and Horemheb," he said, once more assuming the role of lecturing professor.

It occurred to Bracken that Kate must know all, or large parts of this history, on her own. He knew that the University of Texas would not have placed her in charge of this project after Dr. Walker vanished if she were not as every bit as competent as he was. Consequently, she was indeed working her role to perfection by distracting Dr. Walker by playing the part of the starry-eyed undergrad hanging on every word of the all-knowing professor.

"I'll keep an eye on the good doctors, while you get this thing off my hands," Bracken whispered to Platte, trying to position his body in a way that would both hide his hands from view, and allow Platte to use the flashlight on them.

"I continued to find references to this unnamed source of power in records, and they constantly referred to light and flame whenever it was mentioned," Dr. Walker told her, as she slowly moved from where she was standing to keep Bracken and Platte away out of his peripheral line of sight.

Platte maneuvered the flashlight between Bracken's two hands and twisted it. Jake felt the plastic from the zip tie tighten and painfully cut into his wrist, before he heard a slight pop as the zip tie broke. Bracken immediately peered around to see if anyone had heard the zip tie break. Everyone appeared to be oblivious to what they were up to.

"In fact," Dr. Walker continued, "it would seem their discovery was one of the major reasons Horemheb was able to wield power over both Tutankhamun and Ay. I wouldn't be at all surprised to discover Horemheb had used it to finally claim the throne from Ay."

"How," Kate interrupted him, "did they use oil as a weapon?"

"Think of the practical benefits," Dr. Walker encouraged her. "You can use it to light torches to allow your army to move at night. They knew the substance burned, so it's not at all unconceivable that Horemheb's forces learned how to make rudimentary Molotov cocktails, as offensive weapons."

"As the priests were critical to his ability to control the populace, I suspect Horemheb would have divulged his secret to them as well," he paused ruminating over something.

"Some of the documents I found even alluded to the fact that the priest of Ra could command the darkness to retreat in the presence of this new power. Just think of it," he told her, his speech becoming more animated, "the people come to the temple to make their supplication, and the priest, on behalf of Ra, can generate light in the darkness without the benefit of wood or candles. That's no mean trick to pull off, in the name of the Sun god."

"No doubt," he chuckled, "it helped encourage the supplicant's generosity when they passed around the offering plate."

Bracken took the flashlight in his now-freed hands and applied the same process to the zip tie binding Platte. Once again, a barely audible pop accompanied the breaking of the plastic device around Platte's wrist.

"I'm assuming you have a plan?" Platte asked. "If not, I've got one," he whispered over his shoulder.

"Really," Bracken whispered back in surprise. "By all means, let's have it."

"Well," he began, "now that our hands are free, we take your cell phone, and dial up the local constabulary asking for help. Then, we call for pizza. I'm hungry."

"If we can get to it, there are carrot sticks in your backpack," Bracken told him. Platte's only reply he was a muted snort.

"I haven't totally worked it out yet, but" Bracken began in a whisper, "I think we need to wait until the guys move out of the chamber, and they're all closer together, before we divulge the fact that we're untied."

"Did I ever tell you one summer, when I was in college I worked at a photographic studio?" Platte whispered.

"Not that I recall," Bracken answered, letting the surprise of the turn in their conversation show in his whispered reply.

"I'm not sure if you've ever been in a photographic studio, but most of them are well-lit areas for shooting pictures surrounded by chaos. Cables, light stands, and all manner of bric-a-brac scattered in no discernable order. I was a minimum wage assistant to the assistant to the photographer. There were no less than a dozen of us like souls in the place. One day, my assistant for whom I was assisting inquired of me about my apparent lack of enthusiasm for my job."

"He said to me, 'Leon, when anyone else tells an assistant to go find something, they sprint off to do just that. You, on the other hand, slowly walk. Why is that?' he wanted to know"

"And what did you tell him?" Bracken asked, despite himself.

"I told him 'look around this place. Did it ever occur to you they might be running away from what they were looking for, instead of running to it'?"

"And, pray tell, what is the moral to your story as it applies to our current predicament?"

"Sometimes," Platte whispered over his shoulder, "it's not a bad idea to take your time and look around for a bit first."

"Thanks," Bracken said, as he turned his attention back to Kate, "I'll keep that wisdom in mind." He noticed the professor had taken a more carefree stance as he continued his lecture.

"One of these records referred to a unique location for the source of this power," Bracken heard the man say, "unfortunately, the specific location wasn't documented. While it was rather vague, it did allude to the fact this source of power seemed to bubble up from the ground."

"It's nearly impossible to live in Texas without learning something about oil and its vast wonders. One also learns, when groveling to oil barons like Solaris for funds, to acquire some knowledge of their trade before sticking one's hands into their proverbial pockets." He laughed a high-pitched nasal laugh.

"That's one of the unexpected boons of this whole process," he said. "I convinced Solaris to fund my project to find oil they had no idea actually existed." At this Bracken felt Platte tense.

"Down, boy," he whispered to Platte.

"You see, if the oil is bubbling to the surface that usually means a great deal of oil is located just below the surface."

"So, why hasn't anyone found it before?" Kate wanted to know.

"As your friend over there pointed out," he jerked his head back over his shoulder, "there are no known significant oil reserves in Egypt. I guess no one bothered to look."

"So, I took my information to some, shall we say very well-placed friends, in the Egyptian government whom I could trust. I won't bore you with the details, but over the course of the next few years, they worked on their side to create and develop a corporation that could take advantage of my discovery. A corporation, I might add, in which I have procured a substantial number of shares," he smiled ruefully. "My reward for my part in the initial rounds of fund raising," he said, nodding to the trailer.

"If you and you partners are so well-heeled, why are you robbing these chambers?" She asked hotly. If he was insulted by her question, it didn't show.

"Two reasons," he began. "First, locating and exploiting an oil discovery is a very expensive business. These relics," he again indicated the cart behind him, "will fetch a great deal of operating capital in the private shadow market for such rare and unknown antiquities. In fact, we've already circulated a catalog of some of our more spectacular pieces to that very market. The interest, as you might well know, has been astounding."

"And the second?" Kate prompted.

"Ah, yes, the second," he paused to collect his thoughts. "It would seem Horemheb knew and recorded the exact location of the oil field in a document he kept very secret. It was then in turn entrusted to his appointed heir, Ramses the First."

"Ramses feared, correctly it would seem, that all was not copacetic with the people who were sworn to his service. After two years or so, he was deposed and killed in a palace coup. Before he was overthrown, in the ill-founded hope of being able to retake power, he moved all the treasures of his kingdom down here," he gestured to the expanse of the tunnel.

"Problem was, he never got a chance to come back and reclaim it. Over time, Seti, his successor, became too busy with challenges to his own rule, thought his problems stemmed more from the Hittites. "Either way," he continued, "this treasure, including the record of the location of the oil field, was lost to memory."

"It wasn't until you discovered the tunnel's location and the chambers that I was able to deduce where the information I needed had been spirited off to. For that," he said, bowing at the waist and gesturing with a sweeping hand, "I thank you."

When he straightened back up, he reached into his coat and removed a small sealed tube and held it tightly in his hand. "Because it wasn't until tonight, in the last chamber, I managed to find it."

"With this," he went on, "we should be able to locate the field and further the process of becoming very wealthy." Silence the hung in the air as Dr. Walker finished his explanation. Finally, Kate broke the spell with another question.

"Is that why you decided it was time for you to vanish?" she asked him.

"Well, truth be told, I was hoping the investigation into Omar's disappearance would take a lot longer than it did. We," he motioned to the men behind him, "were able to remove a great number of the relics from the preceding chambers during that time," he indicated down the darken tunnel. "After I analyzed the remains of those chambers it became obvious this," he waved the tube, "had to be in this, the last chamber, if it still existed."

"I had planned to work the site with you, through the next round of arrivals, before declaring the dig closed for the season and wrapping it all up."

"However, Dr. Rashid's disappearance, which wasn't planned, caused the Egyptian authorities to seriously consider closing down our expedition for the purpose of carrying out a more detailed search, and investigation, into his absence. If that had happened, my visa would have expired, and I would have been forced to leave the country with the rest of you," he told her. He paused, looking at Kate.

"Anything else, my dear?"

"I do have one more question," she said, as her stance tensed, and her face took on a contemptuous expression.

"Were you responsible for the man who attacked me in Paris?" Dr. Walker paused for a moment, before looking back at her.

"I'm afraid to say that, indirectly, I suppose I was," he told her, with less conviction than he exhibited earlier. "The idea, as I discussed it with my associates, was to prevent the files from getting to the Institute d'Etudes Politiques de Paris. We were concerned that a cleaner rendition of the files would prompt more people to ask questions about the tunnel."

"So, you decided it was worth killing me, just to keep the scanned files from being enhanced?" she asked, with obvious anger in her voice.

"Actually, the idea of killing you never even came up," Dr. Walker told her, obviously uncomfortable. "Our associate, in Paris, was just supposed to steal the laptop. It would appear he was just a little overly zealous in carrying out his instructions. Nothing personal; I hope you understand," he told her with a shrug.

"Nothing personal," she screamed at him, "you arrogant bastard!" taking a step towards him. Bracken could no longer see her face, but knew, just from the tone of her voice, she was furious.

Apparently, Dr. Walker detected the same as she approached him. He quickly leveled Bracken's pistol at her as she took another step forward.

"That," he told her, as he regained his composure, "is far enough." The man standing on the ladder came to Dr. Walker's rescue by saying something to him in Arabic. Dr. Walker glanced to his left and replied in kind. The man halfway up the ladder looked up and spoke something to the man in the chamber above, who immediately began descending the rungs of the ladder.

"And now, it would seem," he told her, stepping back to increase the buffer between them, "question time is over." Replacing the tube inside his jacket pocket as he spoke.

As he did, one of the other men asked him a question, pointing to the ladder. Dr. Walker's answer did not please him; pausing for a moment, he then walked to the ladder, released the extended portion that was sticking up into the chamber, and carried it to the cart.

"We can't leave telltale modern equipment in an ancient tunnel, now can we?" He asked Kate as a matter of explanation.

"You don't have to worry about someone finding a ladder," she told him, anger still permeating her voice. "How long do you think it's going to take them to find the opening we created to the tunnel and discover our bodies?"

"I believe it's going to take longer than you might think," he said to her. She gave him a questioning look, as he continued.

"You see," he began, reaching into his jacket pocket and removing what looked like a remote garage door opener. "I planned from the beginning to cover my tracks. More specifically to wash them away."

"This," brandishing the device, "is a remote detonator. At the other end of this tunnel is a small, but sufficient, amount of C4. We decided from the beginning of our work, once we had cleared all the chambers, to remove the wall of rock, dirt, and rubble holding back the Nile, and allow it once more to flow unhindered back into the heart of the valley."

"Hey," Bracken whispered to Platte, "I think its show time."

"Yea," Platte answered, sounding rather bored, "I was thinkin' they were about done with the previews. Personally, I'll be glad to get out of here. I'm hungry."

"So, you mentioned before," Bracken acknowledged before continuing, "how far is it between here and Kate?" Platte seriously surveyed the distance before answering.

"Three, maybe four strides."

"Here's what we're going to do," he whispered, slowly drawing his legs up to his knees. "Right now, you need to close your eyes so you're better able to see when the lights go out."

"You're not planning on conjuring up any of those ghost things, like that Nazi guy did in that Indiana Jones movie, are you?" Platte inquired, referring to the old, but still popular adventure movie series, starring Harrison Ford. Having learned to trust Bracken implicitly when he directed him to do something, Platte closed his eyes as he commented.

"Once the lights are out," Bracken whispered, ignoring him, "you need to get to Kate, and get her down on the ground. I don't think Walker knows shit-from-Shinola about firing a pistol, much less shooting it in the dark, but I don't want to take a chance that he gets lucky."

"You know," Platte breathed quietly, his voice taking on a serious tone, "once you switch on that flashlight, you're going to be target number one."

"I've given that some thought," Bracken reassured him know. "I'll be right behind you, but I'm going for the good Dr. Walker."

"What about the other guys?" Platte asked.

"I'm guessing they're not shareholders and will haul ass as soon as the shooting starts."

"Just make sure you remember which doctor is which. Dr. Compton has charm, good looks, and wonderful bedside manner. All the things the other doctor doesn't have, except one."

"And what's that?"

"Your 9mm Glock," Platte pointed out. "And as we both know from prior experience, you're not bulletproof."

"So noted. You just keep your eyes shut. When I say go, you get up. Don't open your eyes until you hear the lights go out," Bracken whispered back to him.

"I didn't know darkness made an audible noise."

"Oh, it will this time," Bracken assured him. He again turned his attention back to Kate and Dr. Walker, trying to gauge when to put his plan in action.

"But the authorities will know we came down into, the tunnel and they'll find our bodies." Bracken heard Kate tell him.

"I suppose they will eventually" he paused and smiled, "but you will be the sad victims of a tragic accident. Entering an ancient tunnel to explore it, at the very moment the damn at the other end breaks."

"They probably won't even notice the bruising and blunt trauma on your heads where we knocked you unconscious before we leave. I have a feeling you're going to get pretty tossed about when that massive tidal wave of water finally gets here."

"Cops in Egypt aren't that much different than those in Dallas," he chuckled. "They'll accept the easiest and simplest solution to the deaths of three bothersome Americans, to avoid having to deal with a full-blown investigation."

He turned to one of the men and gave him a command. Because he forgot or because he found a sadistic pleasure in letting Bracken and Platte know what was coming, this time he gave commands in English.

"Knock them out again," he ordered, "then untie them. I'll take care of the woman." The man closest to Dr. Walker reached into the cart, removed a long piece of wood, and started towards the light stand.

"NOW!" Bracken yelled.

Both he and Platte jumped up at the same time. Bracken sprinted towards the wall a few feet away and grabbed the ancient sledgehammer Platte had brought with him and was leaning against the tunnel wall nearby. In what appeared to be one fluid motion Bracken grabbed the ancient hammer, swung it in an arc over his head, and smashed the xenon light that sat atop the light post they had just moments before been attached.

The sounds of shattering glass filled the room as it plunged into darkness amidst a shower of electrical sparks.

Bracken pointed his now illuminated flashlight at Drs. Walker and Compton pinpointing their location for Platte, before dropping it on the ground and stepping away from it simultaneously.

Just as Platte had predicted, Dr. Walker fired an errant shot at the now-abandoned flashlight. As he fired a second round, Dr. Walker was silhouetted for a fraction of a second in the muzzle blast, as if illuminated by a flash of lightning.

It was just enough light for Bracken to make out where Dr. Walker was standing, as he launched himself into the air with his arms outstretched and opened wide. As he tackled his target Bracken wrapped his arms around the man in a bear hug, as the momentum of his impact carried Bracken to the ground on top of Dr. Walker. As the two men hit the floor of the tunnel, he heard Kate scream, and then thump to the ground, and he assumed Platte had carried out his part of the ambush.

As Bracken struggled to position himself for leverage, Dr. Walker brought the pistol up as far as his pinned arms would let him and fired off another shot. The bullet came nowhere close to striking Bracken, but the pistol had gone off a mere inch from the left side of his head. The noise and vibration went through his head with so much force that Bracken momentarily wondered if the man had managed to hit him with a round from the gun.

In an instinctive reflex, Bracken grabbed his head, howling in pain and inadvertently released Dr. Walker's arms. Dr. Walker swung his arm up, and with the flat of the gun struck Bracken on the side of his head, causing him to roll off on the tunnel floor.

He didn't lose consciousness but was dazed as he struggled on his hands and knees. As he did, he heard several people running away, and the motor to the small four-wheeler start. He then heard Dr. Walker yelling followed by the report of the pistol firing off another round in his direction.

The bullet made a loud ping as it ricocheted off the generator. As he made it to his feet, he heard the sounds of the four-wheeler motor diminish into the darkness.

He noticed Platte outlined in the shadow of the flashlight as he bent to pick it up. He shined it towards Bracken and Kate Compton, who was brushing the dirt off her hands, as she moved towards Bracken.

"Are you alright?" Kate asked, appraising his appearance looking at him in the growing flashlight beam as Platte jogged towards them.

"Just dazed," he began, before Platte grabbed Bracken by the arm.

"We gotta get outta Dodge kids," Platte urged forcefully. "I'm not sure how far they gotta go but they do have wheels, and once they get to their exit ramp this guy's gonna blow the dam."

Instead of compliantly moving, Bracken bent forward and put his hands on his knees drawing in a breath trying to clear his head.

"I don't think so," Bracken finally said, as he straightened up. "At least, not without this," he said raising his arm. Platte redirected the flashlight to reveal that Bracken was holding the radio-control detonator in his hand.

CHAPTER FIFTEEN

Valley of the Kings – Luxor Governorate, Egypt

"How in the world did you mange to get that?" Platte wanted to know.

"That was my intention all along, as soon as he showed it to us," he replied. "I'll miss my Glock, but I'm sure I can expense another one. This," he told them, as he put the detonator into his right jacket pocket, "was just a little higher on the list of things we needed at the moment."

"How did you know Dr. Walker was going to flood the tunnel?" Kate asked.

"I didn't know, exactly," he waved his arm around the tunnel, "but, I also didn't think he was going to leave a lot of evidence that he and his cohorts had pillaged the chambers. I thought maybe they would create a cave-in, but that takes a lot more effort on their part and there isn't a guarantee that it would work. It's not something you can just do and be assured it would go as planned. Flooding the tunnel was a fire-and-forget kinda plan," he shrugged. "It was just a guess."

"Pretty damn good guess," Platte said, with a trace of admiration in his voice, as he turned and looked behind him. "I still think it would be a good idea to get outta here," Platte told the pair.

"I agree," Kate piped in. "Are you ok to go on?" she asked, taking Bracken's arm.

"Never better," he told her, as he waved his hand in front of them. Platte led the procession, shining the flashlight in front of them as they retraced their steps to their point of ingress. They weren't running but adopted a jogging pace, definitely faster than it had been on their way in.

"How long do you think we have?" Platte asked, over his shoulder.

"Anyone's guess, but if I had to say, I'd think they opened their access point close to the last chamber, and worked down this way from there," he paused in thought. "That has to be several miles away, or they wouldn't have brought the four-wheeler down here."

"I figure it would depend on how much they value their last load of swag," he considered out loud. "Walker has the map, or whatever it was he needed to find the field. I have no idea what else they took out of there and if they plan to take the time to get it out of the tunnel."

"It's hard to say," Kate told them. "I saw some of it in the cart. They were all nice pieces, and very valuable if sold, but I really wasn't paying that much attention to the individual pieces, I was looking for something I could use to bring you the flashlight I had palmed."

"By the way," Bracken turned to speak directly to Kate. "That was an absolute masterful piece of subterfuge and misdirection, if I've ever seen one. You did a wonderful job." Before Kate could reply Platte spoke back over his shoulder.

"Yes, you did," Platte agreed. "When we get outta here, I wanna talk to you and see if you would care to join a me and my kitty in a not-so-friendly game of poker." Kate looked at Bracken for a clue as to how she should reply. Bracken just shrugged.

"There is another possibility," Platte said, stopping short. "When he realizes the detonator's gone, he might come back looking for it, thinking he lost it when you tackled him."

"He might," Bracken told him, "but I'm guessing he won't. He got what he came for, and his only thought right now is to deliver it to his partners."

"True," Platte mused. "Besides, I bet his buddies, hired hands, have no desire to go anywhere but up and out." As he finished speaking, he started walking again with the others close behind him. They trotted another five minutes, before Kate turned to Bracken.

"What do you plan to do with it?" She asked him, lowering her voice so only Bracken could hear. Without having to ask, he knew what she was referring to.

"I've been wondering that myself," he told her, after a moment's pause. "If Walker manages to get out of here, with whatever it was he found in that last chamber, that document is going to vanish right along with him, quicker than a box of donuts at a FOP Convention," he said referring to the Fraternal Order of Police.

"Did you have to mention food?" Platte groaned.

"Sorry," he said, smiling at Kate as they continued to move down the expanse of the tunnel.

"If the field was as rich as Walker thinks it is," Platte said, stopping again. "And if he can get out of here, a lot of people are going to go to a great deal of effort to help him disappear. They're also going to overlook a few incidental murders to get their hands on a new field."

"Who are they?" Kate wanted to know.

"Anyone in the oil business," Platte told her. "For a new, undiscovered field like that, even Solaris would do a deal with him," Platte answered her, as he turned and continued to walk.

In less than ten minutes the trio found themselves moving up the incline they had gone down when they first entered the ancient tunnel. As they reached the top

Platte stopped and shined the flashlight on the decomposing body of Dr. Rashid.

"What should we do with him?" Platte inquired. Bracken turned towards Kate, who had averted her eyes from the body.

"Does he have a family?" Bracken gently asked Kate. After a moment, she answered.

"No," she finally said, "he was married once, but they divorced a while ago, he told me."

"What do you think?" he turned to Platte.

"Well, emerging like moles out of the bowels of the earth, schlepping a body with a bullet hole is bound to provoke all kinds of questions from people who can put us in jail," he replied, almost immediately. "I vote we let someone else discover him." Bracken eyed the body leaning against the wall for another moment, then nodded his agreement.

With that decided, Platte handed the flashlight to Bracken, and stepped back into the antechamber through the hole in the wall he had breached.

"You go ahead of me," Bracken said to Kate, motioning towards the opening. "I want to make a quick look around and make sure there's nothing here that points to us as being the ones who entered here." She met his eyes and held them for a moment, then nodded and followed Platte.

Bracken made his way back to the body of Dr. Rashid. He glanced at the corpse for a moment and reached into his jacket pocket to extract the detonator. He weighted the device in his hand momentarily before flipping the red protective safety cover up and activating the detonation switch.

Tragedy in Egypt Touches UT

AP Wire Service - The President of The University of Texas, Dallas, Dr. Eric Lasseter, in a news conference this morning, confirmed the death of Dr. Lester Walker.

Dr. Walker, Department Chair of the Archeology Department and Academic Chair Holder of the Solaris Energy Department for Middle Eastern Studies, was leading an undergraduate expedition in the Valley of the Kings in Egypt. This was the fourth year the University had worked on the project located a short distance from Luxor.

"Details are still sketchy at this point," he told the assembled members of the media. "However, it appears Dr. Walker entered a heretofore undiscovered ancient irrigation tunnel in search of his missing colleague, Dr. Omar Rashid, of the Egyptian Department of Antiquities, with whom he worked closely."

"During his search, an earthen dam, constructed some 4,000 years ago, to seal off the tunnel from the waters of the Nile failed, trapping Dr. Walker underground."

During the extensive search and rescue operation mounted by the Egyptian authorities, in which Dr. Walker's body was recovered; the body of Dr. Rashid was also found. It is believed Dr. Rashid became disoriented while exploring the tunnel on his own and died from exposure and dehydration.

Dr. Lasseter announced Dr. Kate Compton, Dr. Walker's assistant, had been promoted to Department Chair. Dr. Compton announced the project was closing down for the season, and a review would be undertaken to determine if the University would return the following year.

Services for Dr. Walker have not been finalized pending the return on his remains. (Story Con't on Page 8)

CHAPTER SIXTEEN

Just outside of Wills Point, Texas

Bracken and Platte were sitting easy on Bracken's front porch. Platte had arrived just fifteen minutes before, long enough to consume half a glass of iced tea, the contents of which was not wholly iced tea.

While Platte was a frequent visitor to Bracken's ranch, albeit a sporadic one, on this occasion, he had ventured out from Dallas at a very curious and odd request from Kate Compton that had reached both men via email.

Neither had seen Dr. Compton for a month.

When the three of them had exited the irrigation tunnel the sun was just coming up marking the start of another day in Egypt. They managed to get back to camp and park the jeep before the camp had stirred to life.

Bracken and Kate were drinking coffee, while watching Platte make a plate of eggs disappear, when a group of day workers rushed into the mess tent, speaking Farsi, French, Arabic, and English all at once.

After a few minutes of confused explanation and pointing, the story finally came out that water had been discovered gushing out of one of the hills to the west of the camp in a rather heavy torrent. Everyone in the tent, including Kate, Bracken, and Platte, followed them out to where they claimed to have seen the water.

Sure enough, when they arrived on the scene, water was issuing forth from the entrance to the irrigation tunnel Bracken and Platte had opened a few hours earlier. Over the next few hours, it slowed and finally stopped altogether, when the water level in the tunnel finally reached parity with the water level of the Nile.

Early in the afternoon trained scuba divers dove on the tunnel. They had only been down for fifteen minutes when one of them resurfaced and reported that they'd found a body. A few hours later, the same divers re-entered the tunnel; although now in the employ of the National Police as opposed to the Department of Antiquities, who had originally summoned them.

In between the change in their employer the three divers removed the body Platte had originally discovered. One of the foremen identified it as being Dr. Rashid. It was another twenty-four hours before Dr. Walker's body was discovered and removed.

The authorities once more halted the progress of the dig while they investigated.

Over the next forty-eight hours, Dr. Compton, Bracken, and Platte were questioned about their knowledge of the tunnel and their whereabouts during the previous few days. One by one each of them skillfully and convincingly lied through their teeth and was cleared to depart a couple of days later.

The three of them took the plane they'd arrived in back to London's City Airport. Just as before, they were taken in a Solaris car, this time a Range Rover, to Heathrow International, where several hours later, they boarded an American Airlines Boing 777 for a direct flight to DFW.

After arriving at DFW, and clearing Customs and Immigration, the trio parted company with hugs, kisses on the cheek, and promises to get together soon.

"I know you claim there's no way to improve on sun tea, but you have to admit, rum does it no appreciable harm," Platte said, taking another long pull from the glass.

"Well," Bracken commented, "it certainly does have a much longer lingering after-effect."

"It also keeps the ice from melting too fast," Platte told him, reaching for the pitcher on the small table by his chair to refill his now empty glass.

Jake had emptied his glass and was filling his battered pipe, when Kate pulled up in front of the house, and parked her car beside Platte's gaudy motorcycle.

Both men rose from their seats when Kate reached the porch, and each exchanged warm hugs with her. As she sat down, Platte handed her a glass of tea. She nodded her thanks and took a big drink from the glass.

"Oh, my God!" she sputtered, lowering the glass and looking at it.

"Get choked on a lemon seed?" Platte smiled at her.

"What's in that?"

"Ah," Platte said. "It's an age-old secret family recipe, handed down from the noble Native American tribe from which my clan descended."

"Rum," Bracken supplied, as he puffed on his pipe.

"And in the proper proportions too," Platte continued, "one to one."

"It's not that I don't like tea, or rum, or even together," she said, this time taking a much smaller sip from her glass, "but I would appreciate a little warning next time." Platte laughed while Bracken continued sucking on his pipe and shook his head.

They spent the next twenty minutes exchanging small talk about what they had been doing since getting back to Dallas. Kate continued drinking from her tea, but in much smaller and slower sips. Eventually, the conversation slowed, then ground to a halt. They sat in silence for a few minutes, before Bracken and Platte looked inquisitively at Kate. Finally, she began talking again.

"Did you see the article about the news conference a few weeks ago in the Dallas Morning News?" Bracken nodded.

"Congratulations, by the way," he told her, "on your promotion." When he said it, her eyes met his, but she didn't reply.

"Well," Platte interrupted, "Walker did have one thing right." Kate and Bracken looked at him. "The National Police did take the easy way out, explaining his untimely demise. No one said a word about bullet holes or C4."

"Did they ever find the other three men?" Bracken inquired. Kate shook her head.

"I don't think they even bothered looking for them. I suspect they knew they were in there but didn't care about recovering the bodies."

"Has any of the swag in the chambers been recovered?" Bracken wanted to know.

"It's hard to say," she shook her head. "The National Police raided a warehouse in Cairo that Dr. Walker had rented, and all the items that were still there have been recovered. But," she paused, "we have no idea what or how much was in the chambers, so we have no way of knowing if we've recovered everything or not."

"We attempted to access the catalog he claimed to have been circulating, but by the time I finally got someone at the University to access his computer files, the website had been taken down."

"Well," Bracken reached over to the table next to him, picked up a manila folder, and handed it to Kate, "maybe this will help." Kate opened the folder, and her eyes widened in disbelief as she flipped through pages.

"This looks like the complete catalog," she pointed to the file. "Where did you get it?"

"Ol' Jake has more culture than organic yogurt," Platte chuckled. "At least he has a lot of friends that do," Bracken continued to slowly puff his pipe before finally speaking.

"I should be able to provide you with as good a set of leads about where some of the pieces went." Kate looked at him with more surprise than she had at the file Bracken had handed her.

"Just keep your fingers crossed that none of the missing pieces turn out to be sad-eyed dogs playing poker, painted on black velvet." Kate laughed then she leaned over and kissed Jake on the cheek.

"Thank you," she whispered. Jake just smiled, and nodded once, before putting his pipe back in his mouth. They sat quietly for a few more minutes, as Kate examined the contents of the folder before he broke the silence.

"What about the map?" Bracken asked.

"No sign of it," she told him. "His clothes were torn to shreds, when they finally recovered his body."

"So," Platte said nonchalantly, "the map, or whatever it was, could still be in the tunnel?"

"It could very well be," she replied. "And if Dr. Walker sealed it up in the tube as well as I assume, he did, it most likely is still there somewhere. If the substrate was papyrus, and the water got into it would have dissolved almost instantly. If it was on sheepskin, it would have been waterproof, but the writing would have been washed off." She paused, trying to make a decision. Finally, she sat up and posed a question.

"I need to ask you both something," she said, looking down at her lap. "Have either of you mentioned anything to anyone at Solaris about the oil field Dr. Walker thought he'd discovered?" She asked quickly.

"No," Platte said dispassionately. As he did so, he glanced at Jake, who removed the pipe from his mouth, and shook his head to indicate he hadn't either.

"I didn't think you would have," relief showing in her voice. "Forgive me, please, but I had to ask. You see, someone has accessed the tunnel since it was flooded." They both looked at her, and Bracken motioned with his hand for her to continue.

"The National Police finally located where Dr. Walker and his gang had entered the tunnel, but it took them quite a while to find it," as she spoke, she reached for a leather case she'd brought with her from her car. As she continued, she removed several 8 X 10 color photos, and handed them to Bracken. As he looked at them, she explained.

"The reason it took them so long to find Dr. Walker's entrance was that it had been very cleverly filled in and disguised to blend in with the surrounding desert." Bracken handed the pictures to Platte. "I sincerely doubt those three guys, even with Dr. Walker's help, would've taken so much time and care," she paused again. "Just like, I also doubt they ever made it out of the tunnel, especially since, Dr. Walker didn't."

"These," she reached back into the case, "are thermal imaged Geo-Sat photos taken of the same area, about a week ago." She handed them to Bracken, then leaned over, and pointed to a spot almost halfway between the area indicated as Dr. Walker's point of entry, and the dig site's camp.

"Notice anything about that spot?" Bracken handed the photo to Platte; pointing out the area Kate had drawn his attention to. Platte studied it for a moment, and then looked back to the first set of photos for comparison.

"This area," he told them, still looking at the most recent picture, "was disturbed not long ago. The thermal imaging shows it to be warmer, which means the area under it, has been exposed to the heat of the sun more recently."

"And this," she told them, handing another picture, directly to Platte, "is a high-resolution photo of the same area again, made just a few days ago. Notice anything?" Platte gazed intently at the picture for a long while before comprehension appeared on his face.

"Someone got sloppy, and stopped too soon," he said, handing the picture to Bracken. He leaned over and pointed to a specific place in the photo, as Bracken looked at it. About a mile north of the area they'd been looking at in the thermal images, the new photo revealed a set of jeep tracks suddenly appearing, as if out of nowhere, in the sand. "It would seem they didn't do a very good a job, of literally, covering their tracks."

"Dr. Walker's partners maybe?" Bracken asked.

"Maybe," she replied, "but there's no way of knowing. Regardless of who they are, it won't do them any good."

"You see, you were right," she pointed to Platte. "There is no oil." Both men looked up in surprise.

"Although I didn't find the catalog Dr. Walker was circulating online, I did find scans of all the ancient correspondences and documents he used to postulate his theory that there was oil in them thar hills," she smiled at Platte. "Or in this case, that thar desert."

Sensing she was waiting for them to digest what she has just disclosed Bracken looked at her and simply said, "Go on."

"Do you know what the Mandela Effect is?" she asked, neither of them in particular.

"Isn't that what Joe Mandela called the punch he used to knock out Sonny Liston in '63, to claim the middleweight title?" Bracken ignored Platte and answered for them both.

"We know what it is, at least in general terms."

"The Mandela Effect is something that falls somewhere between mass hypnosis and *The Twilight Zone*," she explained. "It manifests when the generally accepted understanding about something is believed strongly enough, by enough people, they fail to realize their belief is wrong, even when they later experience the event or circumstance accurately and correctly."

"Everyone thinks, in the second *Star Wars* movie, which in revisionist history, is renumbered to be the fifth, Darth Vader tells Luke Skywalker: 'Luke, I am your father,' when, in reality, the line is 'No, I am your father'," Platte rattled off. Both Bracken and Kate looked at him, with something just short of amazement. "Hey, what can I say," Platte shrugged, "it was on the back the cereal box I was reading at breakfast."

"That's right," she said, regaining her composure and taking up her story anew.

"The term was coined from the first widespread case, which was when the death of Nelson Mandela, the former president of South Africa, was reported in the media in 2013. Most people believed he died while he was in prison in the '80s."

"Something like people seeing what they want to see?" Bracken asked.

"Yes, and no," Kate told him. "It's something like that, but more akin to a widely held and believed false memory. A myriad of people attribute the internet with the rapid rise in such occurrences."

"Would this be the appropriate time to bring up the CIA shooters on the grassy knoll?" Platte wanted to know.

"NO," Kate and Bracken said simultaneously. Platte chuckled, and turned his attention to refilling his tea glass.

"When I discovered Dr. Walker's files, I read the same thing he'd read, and translated it the same way he did. I took it to others in the department, and had them translate it, without the benefit of Dr. Walker's notes or my input. They all translated it the same way Dr. Walker and I had," she paused, and sipped at her glass before continuing.

"But, four days ago, when I looked at the original text again, it suddenly dawned on me it had a completely different meaning than the first times I read and translated it," she said, looking up at Jake. "Granted, it was a slight difference; but that slight difference changed the context and essence of everything in the records."

"So, what did you find?" Platte wanted to know. Bracken was happy just to sit, and let Kate get to the point at her own pace.

"What I found," she began slowly, "when I went back and reviewed it, one more time, was a symbol that indicated where the light from the power everyone was talking about, came from. Or, more to the point, which direction it came from."

"In the original manuscript, the letters between Nefertiti and Horemheb spoke of how they had lit up the night sky, using this new power," she paused, and both Bracken and Platte nodded recalling the lecture Dr. Walker had given Kate in the tunnel. "That's how I read it, and everyone else read it, after we found his research."

"I can't honestly explain why, but I decided to go back and research references to the new power prior to that first mention of it, in Dr. Walker's notes."

"And, what did you find?" Bracken asked, as he tapped out his pipe, and refilled it.

"At first zilch," she confessed. "But for some strange reason, I kept going further back, and looking. I guess you could call it a premonition."

"And, we can assume you found it?" Bracken asked.

"I did," she smiled, sheepishly.

"Let me guess," Platte raised his hand, like a schoolboy. "It leads back to the grassy knoll?" Having learned a little from Bracken about how to cope with Leon, Kate ignored him and continued.

"Please bear with me, but for this to make sense, I need to give you some more background," framing her statement more like a question. Once more, Bracken motioned with his hand for her to continue.

"Tutankhamun's father, Akhenaten, made radical, and very unpopular, changes to the social structure of Egyptian society, when he became the Pharaoh. By the force of his rule, he restructured the religious order of his kingdom. He tossed out all of the gods, whom the people had worshipped for centuries, and replaced them all with one single God: Aten."

"He even went so far as to move the capital from Thebes to Karnack, where he built a massive temple complex devoted to Aten. No one, but especially the folks, whose livelihood was dependent upon the industry surrounding the worship of the other gods, but especially that of Amun, was happy with that arrangement."

"Much wailing and gnashing of teeth?" Platte interjected.

"To say the least," she agreed. "A plot was hatched, more than likely by Nefertiti with the help of Horemheb, to do away with Akhenaten. I found earlier correspondence between the two, speculating on how easily they could control everything, if they forced a succession that would place Tutankhamun on the throne. And that's where I found the first reference to the power of the light that Dr. Walker, and his invested partners and more than a few modern Egyptologists, assumed was the discovery of large oil reserves. They discussed using this power to facilitate the regime change in favor of Tutankhamun."

"The peculiar thing was that they used a different term when they referenced this new power of the light, as being connected to the god Amun."

"At this point, Horemheb was the highest ranking official in the army of Egypt, but apparently not powerful enough in his own right to maneuver the coup they needed, so they decided to enlist the power of the light to assist them. Somewhere around 1355 BC, they pulled it off, and Tutankhamun rose to the position of the Pharaoh."

"And how did that work out for them?" Platte interjected again.

"At first, pretty well," she confirmed. "Aten was demoted to the rank of the other gods, and Amun was returned back to his pre-Akhenaten place in Egyptian culture. Tutankhamen moved the capital back to Thebes from Karnak."

"Ah," Platte said, "I hear a, but then, coming."

"But, then," Kate smiled at Platte, and playfully shook her head, "Tutankhamun came of age and decided he actually wanted to be the Pharaoh, instead of the puppet on the throne.

He began rejecting and resisting the advice and suggestions from both his step-mother, Nefertiti, and Horemheb, who was now the commander of the whole Egyptian army and keeping his own counsel about how Egypt should be governed."

"It's at this point in the timeline that the correspondence Dr. Walker found catches up with the story. But without the prior knowledge of the records from the time of Akhenaten, you don't realize the writing refers to the power of this light coming down to the ground, not up from the ground."

"The Mandela Effect," Bracken said using his pipe as a pointer.

"Exactly," she confirmed. "The symbol, even by itself, clearly refers to the light coming down not going up."

"So, what's the big deal?" Platte wanted to know, still playing the devil's advocate. "Up, down, or sideways, what difference does it make how they used petroleum?" Kate started to answer, but Bracken interrupted.

"How did they get the oil up to be able to make it fall down? The Wright brothers weren't even a gleam in anyone's eye at that point"

"Trebuchet?" Platte offered, using the French word for a siege engine.

"Before the Wrights, but after the Pharaohs," Bracken corrected him.

"OK, I give. How?" Platte shrugged.

"I don't know," Kate said softly. "And it was the power of the light itself, not the power of a liquid they set on fire, to make light. It was a light that came down from the sky. But," she reached again into her portfolio and extracted another photo, handing it again to Platte.

"This," she nodded to Platte's hands, "is from a map composited from the EMAG2."

"Electro-Magnetic Anomaly Grid," Platte interrupted for Bracken, who nodded that he knew what it was.

"Notice this area here," Kate leaned over and pointed to an area on the photo exhibiting a deep red spot. "The dark red color there is an indication of a massive amount of residual electromagnetic activity that has, and for it to be that strong, still does, happen there." Bracken got up, and stood by Platte, looking at the photo for a moment, before looking up again at Kate.

"Where is that spot in relation to other sites around Luxor?" Kate extracted yet another photo and handed it across to Platte.

The EMAG2 map was now overlaid on a Google satellite shot of the Luxor Governorate. The red area sat directly on top of the temple of Amun and within a short radius of the entrance they had opened to the tunnel.

"So," Bracken began, walking back and retaking his seat, "what does it mean?"

Kate simply shrugged and shook her head.

"What it means," Platte said, looking down at the photo, "is maybe your alien buddies really did build the pyramids."

Kate Compton and Jake Bracken looked up directly at Platte. He shifted his gaze from one to the other and with a mystifying look on his face that neither of them had ever seen before.

It was then they both realized that Platte wasn't joking around this time.